The Child in the Tree - 1

& M. A. (

Cover Art by Emmy El

All Rights Reserved

THE CHILD IN THE TREE

Emmy Ellis

M. A. Comley

PROLOGUE

The chill of winter comes to pass,
And I am in here somewhere, still as glass.
One day I will be set free…
Until then you shall suffer with me.

His memory of childhood was hazy before he'd been strung up in the tree. After that, whenever a cruel wind blew, he was reminded of what had happened. What *she* had done, that hideous woman who'd thought nothing of the punishment she'd meted out to him, a teenage boy struggling to come to terms with raging hormones and the fact that his life was a mess. Had it always been a mess?

He rarely let himself remember.

1

From the first time he'd been bound, the metal clasps around his wrists had signalled the beginning of a new life, a new way of thinking and living. She'd made sure he couldn't refuse to do what she wanted. A bribe, as it were. Eventually, she'd destroyed his mind, warped it, and he'd raged at how unfair it was that only he was going through this.

Other boys should suffer, too.

That thought had been the one thing keeping him going during that frigid winter, a new side of himself developing, one that kept talking in his ear, saying what she wanted from him wasn't right. It should be *his* choice, not hers. And now, with another winter fully setting its boots on the ground, him a good few years older, and wiser, and clever, he was about to show Smaltern he was someone they should watch out for. And oh, how the fear of what he was about to do gnawed at his innards and twisted them between sharp teeth. How it hurt. How it spread, a plague of anxiety and wishful thinking that things could be different.

How it forced him to refuse to ever be the child in the tree again.

CHAPTER ONE

Jayden cracked up laughing at his mate, Ben. School was out for the day, and Jayden couldn't wait to get the hell home, although hanging out with Ben beforehand, even though it was colder than a witch's tit, was more of an exciting prospect. They could nip into town and get some sweets, seeing as it was their ritual every Friday, although sadly, Den's wasn't there anymore. The old boy had been killed and his shop turned into a small Poundland. Still, they could go there instead, then go to Jayden's for tea if Ben wanted. He'd ask him in a minute, but he needed to finish their current convo first.

"You can't say *that* to her," Jayden said, nudging Ben in the ribs.

"Why not? She's fancied me for ages." Ben grinned.

He was so much taller than Jayden, looked years older, too, and not someone people thought Jayden should hang around with. He'd heard them say so often enough, and it stung a bit that a 'loser' like him shouldn't be mates with a cool boy like Ben.

What did they know anyway, those kids? It was who you were inside that mattered. That was what Mum always said anyway. The outside was just packaging. It was the heart that counted.

"Yeah, well, going up to her and saying one of your dad's cheesy lines isn't going to get you anywhere," Jayden said, laughing some more.

"Cheesy?" Ben raised his eyebrows, anger souring his face.

Christ, did I say the wrong thing? Go too far?

Ben snorted. "Sod you, Jay. I'm off."

Jayden wasn't sure whether Ben was really narked or not. Maybe he was messing. At least, he hoped he was. "Aww, come on, don't be like that."

Ben strode away, giving Jayden the middle finger. "You're meant to be my bud, man. You know, back me up."

"That's why I told you it was cheesy so you didn't make a prick of yourself."

Ben kept walking across the playground, and Jayden shrugged for the benefit of the onlookers. The last thing he wanted was for anyone to get the gist they'd fallen out, even though it was highly obvious. Jayden had no one else he'd rather be friends with — and, truth be told, no one else wanted him in their circle. He was a nerd, bordering on total geek, so he couldn't blame them.

Jayden followed but at the last minute turned right instead of left. Ben had gone their normal route home, heading for the cliff top, and Jayden would let him be instead of trailing behind him, appearing desperate, even though he was. Desperate and worried he'd lost his only friend. He'd wait round the corner for a bit, giving Ben time to get well ahead.

Down an alley, Jayden leant against the wall and propped one foot up, pressing the sole of his shoe onto the bricks of a house. He got his phone out to waste a few minutes and clicked on the WhatsApp icon, then sent Ben a message: *I'm sorry*.

Ben might reply once he'd calmed down. And if he didn't? Jayden had some serious grovelling to do. Still, he'd do it. Being at school without a friend was shit, and he should know. He'd spent enough years on his own, pretending it didn't bother him, when it had. A lot.

With no response forthcoming, Jayden thought it'd be better to go home this way—he wouldn't accidentally bump into Ben then—so he set off, head down, phone back in his trouser pocket. If he skipped through another alley, he could cut across the park and head to the cliff top that way. He glanced about. It seemed night had come early, what with it already being dark, and he checked his watch. Blimey, only ten past four, but it may as well be nine o'clock.

He entered the second alley, squinting into the gloom ahead, where trees resembled black clouds on sticks, regimented in a line surrounding the park. He couldn't make out the play area, with its swings, roundabout, and high monkey bars, but they were there, lurking in the shadows to his left. A slide with seats beneath it, the benches sheltered by a log awning, drew him to them, and he wandered in the murk, reaching them by instinct.

He sat under the cover, getting his phone out again to check whether he'd missed Ben's message bleep, but there was nothing for him to read. Sighing, he flicked through Instagram, wishing he looked like all the other lads with their nice hair and strong jaws. He'd been blessed with dodgy eyesight, so until he was older and could afford contacts, thick-lens glasses were at home on his face and, much as he'd like to evict them as unwanted tenants, he had no choice if he wanted to see.

The shuffle of footsteps on frost-crisped grass had Jayden lifting his head, and he turned his phone around to light the space in front of him to catch who was coming his way. It might be Ben, and they could clear up their little spat.

Someone stopped beside the slide, only their midsection visible in the meagre illumination. Whoever it was had black jeans on and a dark bomber jacket—so it wasn't Ben. Jayden raised his phone so he could check out the face, but there wasn't one there.

His heart stuttered, and he gasped, his body seeming to melt into a puddle of liquid fear.

Eyes and a mouth surrounded by black wool had given him a bit of a start, and a yelp of surprise chased the gasp, flying out of him. He frowned, his mind scrabbling, and he couldn't think of a bloody thing to say.

"The child in the tree." A man, a growly voice, as though he smoked too many fags or had a bad cold coming. His fleshy lips quivered inside the circular cut-out of the balaclava, cracked from being so dry.

"W-what?" Jayden managed, terror creeping into his belly and sending his legs weaker.

"You're the one I need," the man said, his teeth exposed, giant, brown-stained tombstones in a graveyard mouth.

Need? For what?

"I-I don't know what you m-mean…" Jayden's hands shook, and his phone went to sleep, dousing them in darkness. He scrambled to reignite it, but the fucking thing wouldn't work. It fell out of his hands, and the clatter of it on the concrete pavers told him he'd probably smashed the screen. "Shit!"

Mum was going to have a mare.

A hand clamped around his throat, hauling Jayden to his feet, then the ground disappeared, and he dangled, held up by Balaclava. Head spinning, Jayden tried to draw in a breath, but the hand clenched tighter, and he was carried out from under the slide and across the grass. Bringing his hands up, Jayden clawed at the one around his neck, his attempts at freeing himself useless. Balaclava held him close to his body, so Jayden kicked, his shoe connecting with Balaclava, but the man's grip didn't relent.

Jayden wished he'd gone home the other way now, but thinking along those lines wouldn't do him any good. This bloke had already carried him to the tree line, then farther into the woods, and ever-deeper still, until the trunks and branches became all but invisible in the near pitch-black, and he had no idea where they were going. This way led to the cliff top and home. If Jayden managed to get away, he could run out

8

to the other side of the woods and get Mum to ring the police.

Their trip took ages, all the while Jayden sipping at the air, only a fraction getting into his lungs. He had minimal strength left to fight. As his mind verged on going blank, Balaclava threw him to the ground, and Jayden winced at the sharp pain zig-zagging from his hip to the base of his spine. He gasped, pulling in sweet, cold air, his throat throbbing from being squeezed. His lungs burned, and he pushed to his feet, unsteady on them. With no clue which direction to take, he staggered blindly in circles, hands out in front of him, then stepped forward.

His palms met with material, and he snatched them away, a small whimper scuttling past his lips. "What...?" He didn't know what to say. *What do you want with me? What are you going to do with me?* Neither of those questions had answers he wanted to hear.

"Take your clothes off," Balaclava said.

"Y-you what?" Jayden shook his head, unable to comprehend the order.

"You heard me. You'll suffer like I had to and be grateful for the lesson."

What lesson? And how could he be grateful when he'd been strangled and dragged here? They had to be too far into the woods for anyone to hear him if he called out, so what was the point in trying? "I...I don't understand."

"You will. Now do as you're told."

That voice and its hoarseness grated on Jayden's strung-out nerves, and he shuddered at the thought of removing his clothes. That could mean... No, he wouldn't think that. Not yet. Not until he had to. Like his mum had said, there was no point worrying over things that hadn't happened yet. Sound advice, and he'd take it now, when it mattered most.

If he did what Balaclava wanted, maybe he'd let him go.

But he couldn't bring himself to do it, so he turned and ran, clueless as to whether he headed deeper into the woods or would eventually come out into the park. His legs burned from the effort, but he ploughed on, branches snapping at his face, marking his cheeks with their spiteful wooden fingers.

A tight yank on his hair stopped him, and he jerked in reverse, his back smacking into something. It was the man, his breathing heavy from his pursuit, the hot air of it ghosting over Jayden's cheek then switching instantly to cold.

"Get off me," Jayden said, anger settling into his bones instead of terror. "Fuck off!"

"Swearing will get you nowhere," Balaclava said, then hoisted Jayden over his shoulder and trudged off the way they'd come.

Did I almost make it out of here before he nabbed me?

Jayden pummelled the bloke's back with his fists, kicked and kneed him, but his attempt at hurting him seemed to have no effect. So he bit him, finding only the bomber jacket filling his mouth instead of flesh. Heart galloping painfully, he struggled on, even though it was pointless.

Balaclava dropped him.

Where was he? The darkness was almost absolute here, only the faintest shapes of branches forming a canopy overhead, the trunks closest to him fuzzy, indistinct lines of shadow in the surrounding denser ones.

"Take your clothes off. Do it now before I get really angry."

Something cold and hard brushed Jayden's cheek, and he just knew it was a damn knife. He clambered to his feet and removed his school uniform, and Balaclava tossed some material at him.

"Wear that," he said.

Thankful something truly awful wasn't about to happen—thinking of *that* sent shivers down Jayden's spine—he moved the garment around in his hands to figure out what it was. Woollen, he'd worked that much out. Snagging his fingers on what he assumed was a neck hole, he managed to put the thing on. It was a robe, maybe like the ones monks glided around in, and just to be sure, he patted himself and found a rope belt.

"Do it up," Balaclava said.

Jayden obeyed, confused as fuck and wishing he could get out of this situation without being hurt. But how could he run when it was clear the bloke was going to come after him and bring him back to this spot every time?

His flight response dampened, adrenaline buggering off to wherever it hid when it wasn't needed, and he took the next route—doing as he was told and waiting for a chance to escape. Maybe Balaclava just wanted to beat him up or something, then he'd allow him to go home.

Home. I want my mum.

Jayden's bladder acted up at that, and he willed himself not to piss through being so upset. He scrunched his toes as a distraction and waited for what he had to do next.

Unbelievably, a light snapped on, illumination spilling into the woods in a metre-wide radius, showcasing the mulchy, sponge-like ground, the man from the chest down, and Jayden, the robe the colour of a kiwi fruit's skin and just as furry. The rope belt swayed, the twist of it smooth, and he stared at the knots in the ends. Then he looked at the man—thick-set, about five-ten, black gloves covering clenched fists.

"You're going in there," Balaclava said. "And you won't be coming out until I say you can. You're going to go through what I did. Let's see how *you* like it." He pointed to his right.

Jayden swished his gaze that way, widening his eyes at the tree. Its trunk had the girth of an industrial wheelie bin, the sort that had Biffa on the side and squatted down dingy alleys beside rows of shops. There was a huge circular hole in the trunk, and Jayden wondered how the hell it was still standing. The hole, though, had been cut out, and it yawned, showing off the hollow within. The cut wasn't fresh, and neither was the carved-out inside, but it had been done at some point in the far past, although moss mainly covered the interior now, army-green and dense, its springiness highlighted by a torch hanging from a hook, the beam pointing directly at Jayden.

The round door, or whatever it was, leant against the trunk, a jigsaw piece waiting to be slotted into place to complete the picture. It had four horseshoe-shaped metal arches attached, top, bottom, and two sides, and he flicked his attention back to the tree. Matching arches had been screwed into place there, and padlocks dangled off them. The weather had dulled the metal to almost the same colour as the trunk, and unless anyone was specifically looking for them, the locks wouldn't be spotted.

He was going in there? Inside the fucking tree?

"No," he said, backing away, the ground bouncy beneath his shoes, rendering him unsteady.

"Yes," Balaclava said, coming towards him, fist raised.

He smacked it into Jayden's face, and pain radiated, his nose gushing blood. Tears burned his eyes, and he blinked, opened his mouth, and screamed.

Balaclava whacked him again, and Jayden fell, landing on the ground, the back of his head smacking onto an exposed tree root.

He didn't see or hear anything more.

CHAPTER TWO

In the incident room, Helena stared, mouth hanging, at Evan. He'd been a part of their team for a year now and had settled in nicely. She often wondered what they'd done without him, how they'd coped. He was shit-hot at finding clues on social media and had been a big help to Olivia on that score.

"Say that again?" she asked, blinking in shock.

Evan sighed. "Yarworth wants to give me to the drug unit in the city."

"I thought that was what you said."

Helena didn't get it. The chief had interviewed several people to join this station, picking a final two, and now he was letting Evan go elsewhere, into the waiting arms of another division that would snap him up once they realised how bloody good he was?

"Not fucking likely," she said and turned to face the others. "Did you hear that?"

Andy, Phil, and Ol glanced away from their computers and gave her their attention.

"Hear what?" Andy asked, rubbing his stomach, which was considerably flatter since they'd been going to the gym most weekdays for twelve months.

"Yarworth's on about packing Evan off to the drug unit," she said, ramming her hands on her hips and digging her fingers in until it hurt. "What's all that about?"

Phil shrugged, and Ol groaned.

"We'll see about that," Helena groused.

"He said I'm not needed here after all as there aren't that many big crimes," Evan said, scratching his chin.

All right, she'd agree with that. Since the Walker and Landon cases, nothing much had been going on, but still… "Why bring you here in the first place then? What are you going to do, commute? I can't imagine your wife is going to be pleased about starting a new job again—that's if she can even get one in a school there."

Evan shrugged. "She can home tutor kids if need be."

"And you're happy with this bullshit?" Helena raised her eyebrows. "Seriously, I need you here. I'm going to have a word with that twat and tell him to keep his nose out of our business. I mean, it's not like he's interested in what we're doing anyway, so it shouldn't be a hardship for him."

About to go into her office and phone Yarworth rather than visit him in his, where she'd see his pasty, smug face, she stopped still at her mobile buzzing in her trouser pocket. She drew it out and stared at the screen. Louise. Front desk. Maybe there was something new here they could get their teeth into and prove Evan had to stay.

She carried on to her office, answering the phone along the way. "Good morning to you."

"Same to you. Got a weird one," Louise said.

"Okay…" She shut her office door and walked over to slump into her chair behind the desk. "What is it?"

"I just found a hand-delivered letter in reception. Must have been dropped off this morning. It was sticking out from under the mat at the front door."

"And?" She didn't mean to be so abrupt, but fuck, Yarworth had yanked her chain something chronic. "Apologies. Just had some crap news. Carry on."

"Sorry to hear that. The letter would've made me laugh if what it said wasn't so unsettling."

"Out with it, Louise. Why was it funny?"

"It's an old-fashioned poison pen letter. You know, each letter cut out of a newspaper."

"Seriously?"

"Yep. Want me to read it to you?"

"Go ahead."

Louise cleared her throat. "It's got yesterday's date on it, also cut from a newspaper. There's a poem. Ready? *In the hollow, you'll find him there. If he dies, I do not care. As I suffered, then so shall he. It will bring justice flying to me.* What do you think of that then?"

Chills sprinkled up Helena's spine, and she pressed her free hand to the raised hairs on the back of her neck. "It's a bit vague—I mean, 'hollow'? What the hell does that mean?"

"God knows, but the dying bit...that's not good, is it."

Louise stating the obvious had Helena clenching her teeth. She couldn't take her bad mood out on her, though. The poor cow didn't deserve that, not when Louise and Andy had been getting on so well during their recent dates. The pair of them had a spring in their steps, and it reminded Helena of when she'd first started seeing Zach, the medical examiner.

Had they really been together a year now? Time flew way too fast.

"Erm, no, it isn't good. Maybe it's a stupid joke." Although she couldn't just push it to the wayside. It was an ominous note, no doubt about it, but it could lead to fuck all.

"I don't think so," Louise said. "It says more."

"Okay…"

"Here goes. *He'll be kept for forty-eight hours, then returned from whence he came.*"

Helena's stomach dropped south. "So this implies someone is being held against their will. Have you poked into missing persons yet?"

"No. I wanted to ring you about this first. I'll do it now if you want to stay on the line?"

"Thanks." Helena got up and stared out of the window.

The weather was hideously cold lately, the winter giving a sharper bite than previous years. Snow had been predicted to dump itself on them soon, although she'd believe that when she saw it. Snow this side of Christmas didn't seem likely nowadays, climate change farting around with the seasons and mixing them all up so the white stuff tended to make an appearance a month or so before spring.

A man walked along the street, hands shoved into his bomber jacket pockets, his shoulders hunched to warm his ears. He stopped and turned, staring at the station, seeming to take it all in then stopping his perusal at her window. She gazed down at him, barely able to make out any features, but his black-as-coal hair and eyebrows were a stark contrast to his overly pale face. He lowered his shoulders, straightening them, and glared, then smiled, throwing his head back as though laughing.

"Fucking weirdo," she muttered.

"What was that, guv?" Louise asked.

"Nothing." She almost blushed at being caught talking to herself.

"Right," Louise rushed out on a breath. "Officers were called round to the home of a lad last night. He didn't come back from school yesterday, and his parents rang in about nine p.m. after phoning around to see if anyone had seen him. Uniform have had a look round the house, asked the usual questions, but nothing much else has been done. There's a note here that says the lad had a bit of a to-do with his friend, a Ben Griffin—they usually walk home together but didn't yesterday."

"Okay, what's the missing kid's name?"

"Jayden Rook, thirteen. The parents have tried ringing him, but it's gone straight to voicemail."

"Hasn't his phone been pinged?" Helena asked.

"Not that I can see in the log."

"Fucking great. Okay, set that in motion for me, will you. And get that hand-delivered note to forensics. Tell them you've touched it — I presume you didn't put gloves on."

"No, I didn't. It just looked like a pamphlet folded in half, one of those flyers for house cleaning services and the like."

"Never mind. What's the boy's home address?"

"Sixteen Bladen Street."

Up on the cliff near where she'd been held by Uthway in the storage container. Although time had passed, she still had an aversion to going up that way, but unfortunately, she had no choice today. "I'll get Andy to go there with me now. Despite uniform doing jack shit, I'll get the rest of the team on it. We haven't got much else on, and it can't hurt for us to work on it." *May as well make use of Evan while we still have him.*

"Okay, guv, I'll get back to you about Jayden's phone."

"Can you repeat the poems to me so I can write them down?"

Louise did that, and Helena thanked her then slid her phone away. She walked to the incident room and stood in front of the whiteboard, a piece of paper from her notepad in hand.

"Guys, this might not be anything, yet it's definitely something off." She waved the paper and explained about the poison pen letter, Jayden Rook, and then read out the poems. "So, this could be related to him or it could just be a coincidence that a kid's gone missing the same day the note was crafted."

"Why bother with the faff of cutting out newspaper clippings these days?" Ol asked. "People are better off using computers and printing these sorts of notes out."

Helena shrugged. "No idea. Maybe he's been watching too much *Poirot*. Either way, we can spend today on it and see if it takes us anywhere. As you know, I don't like how we have to operate with missing persons—and I suppose at thirteen, Jayden isn't considered young enough to have us all out there searching yet. You know how it goes: angry kid walking off so it sends a message to his parents; he went to stay with a mate without permission; he has a bad home life so felt he could just swan off and come back when he's had enough. Meanwhile, in these instances, some kids are actually in danger. So we're going to treat it as though he is, okay? If it turns out he's not, good, but in the interim, we'll get cracking."

"Most kids his age avoid Facebook," Ol said.

"Instagram is the best bet," Evan supplied.

"Get on with it then. Phil, do your usual with CCTV. Concentrate on the roads around the school—and it would bloody help if I'd asked Louise which one he goes to, seeing as some of them go to the one in the city." She turned and wrote Jayden's name and address on the board.

"I'll do it now," Ol said.

"Thanks. Poke about with this info" — Helena tapped the board — "and see what we get. Andy, we're going to visit the parents and get their measure. Oh, and Louise is sorting a phone ping. I'll ask her to let you know as well as me when she's got something."

With Andy in tow, less of the huffing and puffing coming from him now he was fitter, they went down to the front desk. Helena asked Louise to ring the team with any phone info, then they headed out into the car park. Engine revving, Helena buckled up, and they were off, driving towards the cliffs.

The recollection of jumping from it into the sea flitted through Helena's mind, and she tried to bat it away, but it insisted on playing out, as per usual. It didn't stop until she'd swum to the shore and flagged down the help of that woman walking her dog. She shuddered at the emotions it brought on — fear, the heady thrill of freedom, and the idea that Uthway would come back for her soon and finish what he'd started — selling her to the highest bidder in a sex slave scam.

"Are you all right?" Andy asked, as usual ferreting in the glove box for a Werther's. "Fancy one?" He held up the golden-wrapped piece of Heaven and waggled it.

"No, thanks." She hadn't eaten one since the last time she'd chomped at it in anger and Andy had commented on it.

"Gone off them, have you?" He popped the sweet into his mouth.

"No, just don't feel like it today. I need to cut sugar out," she lied.

The climb to the cliff didn't take long, and she avoided looking at the expanse where metal storage containers sat row upon row in an area she wished didn't exist. She turned onto the estate and drove towards Bladen Street, wondering whether the lad was home now and his parents hadn't thought to ring it in. And if he wasn't? Jayden being out overnight bothered Helena, and if the note was to be believed and it was connected to Jayden, he wouldn't be released until after school tomorrow.

If he was being held, why?

That's what I aim to find out.

She pulled up outside number sixteen and cut the engine. Andy crunched his sweet, so to save having a go at him about it—God, she hated loud eaters—she got out and waited for him on the path. While he undid his seat belt, she took a good gander at the house. Detached. Maybe four bedrooms. A wide drive with privet hedges either side. This wasn't the home of some unfortunate teenager who had hard times—on the outside, at least. Inside might prove her wrong, as would the parents and how they behaved, but her gut told her for this kid to be missing, it was a genuine case of him falling foul of something — or someone.

Andy joined her, and they walked up the drive. The front door opened, and a woman stood there, her face showing signs of her not sleeping the previous night. Bags camped beneath her red-rimmed, puffy eyes, and her mottled cheeks, as well as her eyes, gave away the fact she'd been crying recently. Her blonde hair had been shoved into a messy ponytail; it hung limply to one side, as it should when this mother had more important things on her mind.

At the door, Helena showed her ID and introduced them. "And you are?" *Damn me for not asking Louise.*

"Katherine Rook," she said, nervously fiddling with the hem of her long T-shirt that appeared as though she hadn't taken it off since yesterday. "Come in."

Helena and Andy stepped inside and joined her in a spacious living room. A black leather corner sofa took up one end, and a huge TV hung above a fire that had no mantel — one of those electric screen-type efforts with fake flames. A recliner chair sat beneath the window, and heavy, expensive red velvet curtains were held back by fancy metal holders screwed into the wall. All in all, the home of someone well-to-do, but Katherine didn't strike Helena as the posh sort. New money, maybe, earned from hard work, not passed down from someone else's coffers.

"Please, have a seat, Katherine," Helena said. "Would you like Andy to make you a cup of tea?"

Katherine moved towards the door. "Sorry I didn't offer one. I'm all over the place at the moment."

"I'm sure you are. Would you prefer to make it? Maybe it'll calm you while we talk? We can go into the kitchen, if you like."

Katherine nodded and led the way. The kitchen was high-gloss and trendy, mainly duck-egg hues with black cabinets and worktops. Katherine poured coffee from a three-quarters-full carafe, and Helena helped her carry the mugs over to the table. While Helena and Andy sat at the island in the centre, Katherine went to the fridge and took out milk. She brought over a tube of sweetener, a spoon, and set the milk down.

"Help yourselves," she said, sitting opposite them. "Have you heard anything yet?"

"We're not sure," Helena said. "If we could have a little chat, things might become clearer. Now, as you've already noticed, we haven't got moving regarding Jayden not returning home for a variety of reasons. Once he's been gone forty-eight hours, we ramp things up, but his age brings lots of factors to the table — many teenagers go off for a while then return home of their own accord. However, I'd like to pursue his disappearance myself in the time between uniforms treating it more seriously."

"Okay…" Katherine added two sweeteners to her cup then poured milk.

"So, if we can get a bit more information on what Jayden's like, what his homelife is like, things of that nature, it helps us to build a picture of where his mind might be at. Some questions might be upsetting, but think of it as us doing everything we can to find him, rather than us casting aspersions, okay?"

Katherine nodded.

Helena sorted her coffee then smiled. "Let's start then, shall we?"

CHAPTER THREE

"You need to go to your grandmother's," Mum said from in front of the kitchen sink.

His guts rolled over. He hated going there, where the old bag spouted stuff about God and Jesus, trying to get him to go to church with her and have his sins absolved. He didn't want to go to bloody church, and he didn't want to hear all the verses from the Bible either, but she'd read them out to him all the same, the book perched on her lap like a splayed-open black crow, the front and back covers the wings, the pages the rancid guts.

"Do I have to?" He sounded whiny, but blimey, he couldn't help it. "You know I don't like her." And that was an understatement.

Mum grimaced, her hands and wrists obscured by washing-up suds. She ferociously attacked a saucepan that had contained baked beans, her scrubbing brush scraping on the bottom, water sloshing with every back and forth. "I don't much like her either, love, but with your dad gone, we're all she has left."

He hated being reminded that Dad was 'gone'. Why couldn't she just say he was kicking up daisies; dead; in Heaven – anything was better than 'gone'. Dad snuffing it last year had been a massive blow, purposely taking himself away from them and leaving Mum to struggle. Grandmother – she didn't like gran or nan, what with having airs and graces she couldn't back up with a pedigree – expected him to go round there every other night after school and be instructed in the ways of the Lord.

Mum reckoned if he did that, Grandmother would keep helping them out. The old dear was rolling in it and could spare a few quid here and there to put towards the weekly shop. So he did it for Mum, for them, but still wished he didn't have to.

He left the kitchen to put on his coat in the hallway, the collar cold from where he'd not long got in from school. It was nippy out there, and he didn't fancy traipsing the streets on a Friday to the cliff top where Grandmother lived in her fancy six-bed and only her there to fill the space. He'd asked her once why she didn't let them move in, and she'd snapped that she didn't want his sinful backside in her home for any longer than necessary.

Why, then, did she insist on the sodding Bible study if she didn't want him there?

After going way past the estate towards the few houses about half a mile out, he didn't go to Grandmother's house. Instead, he turned at the end down the side of Mrs Zadolka's so he could walk over the cliff top and take a moment to balance on the edge where Dad had once stood for the final time. People didn't think he knew, but Dad had thrown himself off after losing his job and being down in the dumps for months, no thought of how his wife and kid would manage without him.

He hated him for that.

With the toes of his shoes peeking over the edge, he let the wind smack into him and the cold air snap at his cheeks and the tops of his ears. The weather had been much the same the year Dad had been there, and he imagined how his father must have felt, in this very spot, knowing the dark, choppy sea would snatch him down into its watery belly and keep him there until it saw fit to spit him out onto the rocks, partially digested and bloated.

A shiver rattled down his spine, and he closed his eyes, dicing with death, rocking backwards and forwards, daring a brisk wind to kick up and shove him off the ledge. It didn't, so he took a step back then peeked over. The sea churned, wave tops wiggly lines of frothy spume, and he had to admit, it was enticing. Mum would be better off without him to feed and clothe, and maybe she could start again without having him as a ball and chain.

She'd be gutted if he ever told her how he felt.

So he didn't follow in his father's footsteps, he turned around and made for Grandmother's, all the while thinking of how she'd preach to him in her imperious voice and expect him to believe everything that came out of her flabby mouth.

He might have believed in God at one point, but what sort of God took his dad away, eh? He thrust that out of his mind – getting annoyed wouldn't make for a pleasant visit. Not that they were ever pleasant, but...

At the bottom of her gravel drive, he shook his head at the ridiculousness of her home. A family belonged in it, not some decrepit old biddy. The walls should echo with the tinkle of laughter, not throw back her teachings about John, Mark, and the like, her tone crackling with something akin to brimstone and fire.

He stomped up the drive, deliberately heavy-footed so he created dips in the stones. She hated that, as did Mrs Zadolka. Why have gravel then? He smiled at the thought of Grandmother watching him, raising a fist and muttering that he was an imbecile. She loved that word. It might as well be his name.

The door swung open, and the beefy cow stood on the threshold, meaty hands on fleshy hips, her thick lips parted, ready to spew hatred, no doubt.

"You're late again," she said, sounding like she was sucking a plum.

"Yeah," he said.

"It's 'yes', not 'yeah', you cretin."

31

He used to be hurt by her name-calling, but each one rolled off his back now. Mum had asked him to grin and bear it, so he'd do it for her. Mind you, once he got to eighteen, he wouldn't come here to see her. No one could tell him to do it then, not when he was a man who had rights.

She stepped back to let him in and watched, hawk-like, while he removed his shoes and placed them just so in the cupboard on the far wall of a hallway bigger than his bedroom. He hung his coat up, too, then closed the door and turned to find her holding out the slippers she expected him to wear. They'd belonged to Grandad – it had been okay to call him that when she hadn't been within earshot – but he was deader than Dad, having passed of a heart attack about ten years ago.

Holding back a sigh, he put them on, and she nodded her approval and led the way to her 'drawing room', which was really just a normal room she'd given a fancy name to. Inside, a black piano, unused since Grandad wasn't here, gave it a posh feel, as did occasional tables scattered about, home to all sorts of weird knickknacks that were dusted daily by the cleaner who came by in the mornings.

Mum did the cleaning in their house as well as other people's.

Resentment built, and he stared at the strange ornaments, a mix of Egyptian people in mad poses, and ducks, dogs, cats, and birds. Plus, of course, the large statue of Jesus that had always freaked him the hell out. It was painted, the robe a mossy green with a rope belt, the guy's toes poking out from beneath the hem. His hands, held in front of him, bore the signs of stigmata, the blood lifelike and a bit unnerving. It was the eyes that did it, though, that brought on the shivers. Jesus stared, maniacally, as though he had more than conjuring bread for the five thousand on his mind.

"Sit down," Grandmother said, pointing a sausage finger at his usual chair, the one right next to the freaky Jesus on his very own table, a pedestal.

He swallowed and did as she'd asked, then waited, as usual, for her to leave the room. Same as every other time, she came back bearing a silver tray with two golden goblets on it, plus two white wafers. She'd do what she always did and force him to eat the body of Christ and drink the whatever the hell it was, then she'd babble on until what she said went in one ear and out the other.

He wasn't even Catholic.

"Today we're going to do something different," she said, placing the tray on the only table that didn't have any weirdness on it.

He nodded.

"We are going to teach you a lesson."

He didn't need to ask who she meant by 'we'. It was her and Jesus and God. The three of them would try to bend him to their will, but he wasn't having any of it.

"You're going to be Jesus himself," she said. "Strung up on the cross."

If she expected him to play-act, she could fuck right off.

"How's that going to work?" he asked.

"Drink that, and you'll see."

She pointed to the goblets, and he lifted one, the scent of the usual 'blood of Christ' wafting up. He necked it, hating the taste, and swallowed, the cool liquid wiggling down into his stomach.

While he waited for her to say something, to read from the pages of the crow, things got a bit woozy. He blinked, trying to keep his eyes open, but the damn things wouldn't obey. He sat back, head bobbing, and rested it on the chair.

Sleep came knocking and whispered for him to follow it down into the depths, and among those whispers were Grandmother's, telling him she'd teach him a lesson and no mistake, and when he woke up, he'd know what she meant.

CHAPTER FOUR

Jayden came to in the darkness, his arms out at his sides and up, as though pinned in place. He tried to move them, but bands or something held him captive. His armpits ached, as did his neck where he assumed he'd been asleep with his head hanging. Talking of hanging, he seemed to be doing just that—his feet weren't touching anything solid below, and his shoes didn't feel right. And that smell—God, it was gross. Musty, earthy, as though he was outside.

Then he remembered. Sitting beneath the slide. That bloke coming along in the balaclava. Being carried into the woods. And the tree with the hole in it. Christ, he was in there, wasn't he, secured to the inside by something that chafed his skin.

He called out, his voice croaky, then tried again, louder, his plea for help more urgent. Desperate. Pleading. The words sounded muffled, going nowhere—maybe it was the confined space—so he yelled again, louder, pushing his words out through dry lips. He licked them and winced at the sudden sharp pain. They were split, and he recalled Balaclava smacking him one and knocking him out. The back of his head throbbed, as if to remind him he'd fallen on that tree root, and he groaned with too many sensations and realisations hitting him all at once.

Panic promised to overwhelm him if he didn't get a handle on his emotions.

Would anyone even hear him through the circle door? He thought back to when he'd first seen it and roughly calculated the thickness of the cut edge. Maybe six inches or so—six inches separating him from someone out there who could help. People walked their dogs in these woods, so surely he'd be heard if he kept shouting.

Wouldn't he?

He did that for a while until his voice grew hoarse, his throat sore, then wiggled his fingers to get some feeling into them. They'd gone slightly numb. Something brushed the fingertips to his left, and he wafted them again. A featherlight *thing* rested on his palm, and he manoeuvred it until a heavy weight knocked on the heel of his hand. String with a metal ball on the end? That was what it felt like. He tugged, and a light came on, close to his cheek, blinding him. He turned his face away and blinked until he could stand the harshness, then moved his head to inspect the light through the smeared lenses of his glasses. What was on them? Dirt?

A battery-powered brass lantern hung beside his head, and he glanced over to the other side of the hollow where the torch from earlier had been, but it had disappeared. Balaclava must have taken it with him.

A large piece of paper had been tacked to the tree-wall opposite, a message written in capitals with a thick black marker: *The light won't last forever, so use it wisely.*

Jayden stared at the bonds in turn. There was no way he'd be able to free himself. They were metal circles with chains coming off them, the ends of which had been attached to the wall on little silver, square plates. There were only five links, so he didn't have much room for movement. His wrist skin was red, and angry-looking divot lines marked where the cuffs had dug in while he'd been out of it. But it was his palm that brought on a rush of fear. It had blood on it in the centre, bright red, as did the other one, and that couldn't be right. It should be dark brown by now, having dried in the time that had passed since he'd been strung up in here.

Was it fake?

He swallowed, dread sending his heart pattering, and he glanced up, wanting to take in all of his surroundings before he switched the light back off. The ceiling, if he could call it that, was about half a metre from his head and rounded; he was inside a wooden dome.

What sort of man was Balaclava to have done this? A maniac, and then Jayden asked himself the question he'd been keeping at bay.

What was Balaclava going to do to him next?

He wet himself, the fluid hot as it meandered down the insides of his legs. He gazed south, and his stomach rolled over. Instead of his shoes, old-man slippers had taken their place, tartan affairs that appeared worn, and they were too big, meant for a man with large feet. Green garden twine held them on him, wrapped around the front, but the backs hung low.

Then, as if it had been waiting for just the right moment, the cold made itself known, his wet legs springing goosebumps, the scent of his piss billowing up. He gagged, and his eyes watered—not just from the stench but terror, ripe and wicked, and it engulfed him, spreading through his body until he shook and couldn't stop.

Remembering the note, he managed to control his quivering hand enough to grasp the light pull and tug it. Darkness came, shocking and frightening, and while he knew what his surroundings were like, that knowledge disappeared, replaced with a scarier place, Jayden in a scabby, upstairs room somewhere, with Balaclava downstairs, plotting the second stage of his plan.

Jayden closed his eyes and willed himself to go to sleep, but his mind wasn't complying. It preferred to encourage his thoughts to spiral, and he almost drove himself mad watching the flickering images of him being tortured, those fat lips and beady eyes hovering in front of him behind the black woolly mask.

Mercifully, he wore himself out, and while he drifted off, he wondered whether the cold would kill him, saving Balaclava the job.

CHAPTER FIVE

He'd taken a few days off work to do what had to be done. Grandmother might be dead, but she still spoke to him, and he listened. He'd finally succumbed to her teachings once she'd made him Jesus in the tree, too scared to disobey her in case she put him in there again. It had wrecked him, those two days inside the trunk, that nasty robe itchy, his wrists so sore from the metal cuffs.

He'd replaced them for the boy. The old ones had gone rusty over the years, and flakes had drifted off them when he'd gone inside to get it ready for him. He'd given the kid a light, which was a damn sight more than he'd had, and he hoped it wouldn't mess things up. Maybe he shouldn't have been so kind. The lesson might not work if he changed things, and the boy may not be willing to learn the ways of the Lord if his time there was too comfortable.

He should have listened to Grandmother, but his kinder side had told him to do otherwise.

Two days of being hungry, thirsty, abandoned, and terrified should do the trick, though, with or without the glow from the little brass lamp.

He was surprised the kid going missing hadn't made the news. Perhaps his parents were used to him going off by himself and hadn't called the police yet. It didn't matter if the coppers had been told. No one would be able to find him anyway. They could search all they wanted but would come up with fuck all.

Leaving his house, the one handed down to him by Grandmother, he strolled off to the cliff top and did his usual dice with death. Then he sat on the cold grass and pulled the boy's phone out of his pocket. He'd found it beneath the slide, no PIN needed to give him access, and had removed the battery and SIM so it couldn't be tracked. That was what the TV programmes said to do anyway.

Now, he replaced them, turned it on, and quickly opened WhatsApp. The last message had been to someone called Ben, so he tapped out a new one: *Help me! I'm trapped in the hollow!*

The bad side of him laughed his head off at that, then he powered the mobile down, removed the battery and SIM again, and slid it all into his pocket. Hurriedly walking away from the location, he entered the nearby estate and found himself in his old street. It looked as it had in his youth, bar being slightly shabbier, litter gathering in crowds along the edges of the pavement, having a rustling natter as the wind blew. Wheelie bins now took the place of black sacks waiting for the rubbish collectors out in the gardens, and several cars lined the kerbs, flashier than in his childhood, despite the estate being renowned for having the scabbiest arse in town.

Outside his previous home, he smiled, imagining Mum inside, washing up or hoovering, maybe polishing with a yellow cloth when she had more time instead of flicking the feather duster about. She'd moved away a while back, having met a new man, and he was glad for her. Smaltern held too many bad memories, and since he'd taken to going to church, she'd grown distant with each passing year. They rarely spoke, and he couldn't even remember how old his little siblings were, the ones produced in a better marriage in a better town. A better life.

She hadn't wanted anything to do with Grandmother's house or money once the old bat had died.

It suited him. They were his rewards for putting up with the dragon for as long as he had. He wanted to renounce his faith at times, to walk away from it all and be who he'd been before, but that tree...those forty-eight hours...the cellar...Grandmother chattering to him even though she was six feet under. No, he couldn't turn his back on the church, despite how much he wanted to when his good side explained that his actions and thoughts regarding the hollow were wrong.

If he did walk away from God and Jesus, the Devil would get him. Grandmother had promised him that.

"If you were a true Catholic," she said now, standing beside him as though alive and breathing, "you wouldn't have put that child in the tree."

He raised his eyebrows at that. "Pot calling the kettle black?"

Why the change of heart? Why tell him to do it if she was going to make him doubt himself?

"Be quiet," she huffed. "Do as I did and get on with it. I was merely musing on what others would think of our behaviour. What Father Pinto would say. He'd be so very cross and wouldn't understand."

He ignored her, tempted to return to the woods and check on the boy again like he had earlier, but if he did that, he could ruin everything. He had to wait the full forty-eight hours from now on, then he could explain to him that going to church would save him.

It struck him then, that had he not poked around on the lad's phone, he wouldn't even know the kid's name.

Jayden.

He would suggest he changed it when they had their little talk.

"What a jolly good idea," Grandmother said. "Jesus is so much more appealing, isn't it?

CHAPTER SIX

"Jayden is a good lad," Katherine said. She pulled her phone across the table and accessed her photos. "There he is, look."

Helena studied a boy who reminded her of Harry Potter, minus the scar on his forehead. He wasn't the trendy type of youth she'd expected, someone who seemed able to take care of himself at a pinch. No, this kid was still too immature, going by his face, although that could be deceiving. Maybe he was more worldly-wise than Helena was giving him credit for.

"Lovely," she said, a pebble-sized lump expanding in her throat. "You must be very proud of him."

"I am." Katherine's eyes watered. A tear fell, and she dashed it away with the back of her hand.

"Do you have a recent picture we can take with us?"

Katherine pointed to one in a silver frame on a beechwood sideboard.

"We'll bring it back as soon as we get it scanned and printed off — unless you can do that for us?" Helena asked.

"I have another in the top drawer there. School photos." Katherine gestured for Helena to fetch it herself.

She did, feeling bad for rooting around even though she had permission, and placed it on the table.

Katherine stared into space, another tear dribbling down her cheek. She didn't bother getting rid of it. Its journey took it to her jawline, and it hung their briefly then plopped off to land on her chest, creating a tiny wet patch the size of a baby's fingernail. "He wouldn't walk out, you know. He's not that sort of kid. He hangs out with Ben and that's it. He doesn't get into trouble in school or out of it. A grades. I don't understand how the police last night could possibly think he's gone off for a laugh, as they put it. A *laugh*? Jayden wouldn't find that funny. He just wouldn't do it. And I *know* something's happened to him." She formed a fist over her

48

heart. "I can bloody *feel* it." Her bottom lip wobbled.

Helena was livid about what the officers had implied. What the hell had they been thinking?

"I believe you," Helena said. She did, too; there was no bullshitting a fraught mother going on. This was way off, and what with the note... As for the officers saying he'd gone off for a laugh... She'd be having words with them about watching how they put things in future. Jesus.

Helena pressed on. "What about Ben? I have information that tells me Jayden sent him a message yesterday after school."

Katherine nodded. "About fifteen minutes after their little row, although Ben says it wasn't anything that serious. Ben had just got the hump over something Jayden had said, and they didn't bother going to get their sweets like they usually do—that's their thing on a Friday after school, spending pocket money." She swallowed. "Ben walked off, and he doesn't know whether Jayden waited before following him."

"He attends Smaltern Secondary, I take it?" She had to ask in case he went to the school in the next city over. Smaltern was growing, and the schools were only able to accommodate so many.

"Yes." Katherine sniffed.

"Andy, will you give Louise a ring and ask her to send a couple of uniforms down the school and get some questioning started?"

He bobbed his head and left the room.

"So you really *do* believe me then?" Katherine stared across the island, wide-eyed.

"I do. The sooner we get things in motion, the sooner we can find out where he is and get him back for you." Helena smiled, hoping that would be the outcome but worrying it would be a different scenario altogether. If his disappearance *was* connected to the note, the former might come true by tomorrow evening. "So, Jayden sent a message. What did it say?"

"*I'm sorry* — that was it. Ben said he was going to reply later when he'd had a chance to cool off, but with homework, then dinner, and a film he wanted to watch on telly, he forgot so planned to catch up with him today at school. Then I rang his mother to see if Jayden was there, and the rest..." Her voice quivered.

Helena reached out and squeezed the woman's hand. "We'll do everything we can to find him, I promise. What about Jayden's father?"

"What do you mean?" Katherine frowned.

"Are you with him? Is he at work?"

"William? Oh, he's in Afghanistan."

Shit. "And have you told him Jayden is missing?"

50

"I tried ringing last night, but where he is, communication is spotty at best." She stared out through the patio doors, maybe visualising scenes of happier times when the family of three had been out on the grass, having fun in the sunshine. "I thought Jayden would be back and Will wouldn't need to know anything about it until we next spoke."

"Probably the right thing to do," Helena said. "He can't do anything from out there, and worrying him seems cruel, considering what he's doing in Afghanistan. Now, this question is possibly going to be a bit alarming, but I have to ask, and believe me, I wouldn't if I didn't have to." Helena took a deep breath. "Do you know of anyone who would want to abduct or hurt Jayden?"

Katherine's eyes scrunched shut, then she opened them and turned, staring directly at Helena. "Absolutely not. I told you, he's a good boy. There's no one in our family or even friends who would take him away. I can't even begin to imagine who it would be."

"Okay. Are there any grudges in your past — yours or Will's?"

"What, you think it could be connected to *us*? That they've taken Jayden to pay us back for something?" Katherine's hand fluttered at her neck.

"We have to look at all avenues, I'm afraid. An investigation like this means turning over all sorts of ancient stones, as it were. Do you recall anything that is likely to bring on this sort of revenge?"

Katherine's eyes shifted from side to side, as though she frantically sought an answer—even seeming to will a grudge into play so there would be something to latch on to. "I can't think… There's nothing coming to mind."

Then this might be a random grab.

"Do you have any other children?"

"No."

Andy came back in and nodded.

"We'll need to take a look in his room," Helena said.

"The police already did that last night." Katherine rose and walked towards the door.

"I know, but we may spot something they missed. It's best to be on the safe side, yes?"

"Absolutely," Katherine said, seeming to relax despite the circumstances. Maybe because she could see things being done, rather than wondering what was happening.

Helena and Andy followed her upstairs. Jayden's room was a double, spacious and tidy, nothing like the usual teenager.

"Did you do a spring clean in here since yesterday or something?" Helena asked.

"No, this is the way he keeps it. The police told me to leave it exactly as it is, so I did." Katherine smiled sadly.

Helena stepped inside. "You don't have to stay if it's too painful watching us work. Some people find it hard seeing strangers going through their children's things. If we find anything, we won't take it unless we've told you first."

"I'll...I'll just go...go to the bathroom." Katherine walked away, weaving unsteadily. Then came the sound of the lock snapping into place and the wail of a mother crying out her pain.

"Christ," Helena whispered, shaking her head.

Andy came in, too, and they got on with it, opening drawers with gloved hands, checking inside the built-in wardrobe with its opaque white doors and getting down on hands and knees to peer beneath the perfectly made bed.

Army standard. Had his dad taught him how to clean a room?

There was absolutely nothing that shouldn't be there or would give them a clue.

"We're shit out of luck," Andy murmured.

"So what's new?" she shot back wearily.

They walked out onto the landing.

"We've finished," Helena called.

Katherine opened the bathroom door and came out, her cheeks red, her eyes puffier than when they'd arrived. Helena's heart broke for her, and if it was the last thing she did, she'd find Jayden and bring him home — dead or alive.

"Do you have anyone who can come and keep you company?" Helena asked while they trooped down the stairs. At the bottom, she waited by the front door, eager to get away and begin the search for a child who'd seemingly vanished into thin air.

"No," Katherine said, coming to stand in front of her, entwining her fingers as if that would stop them shaking. "I don't want anyone here. I can't cope with the fuss, the sympathy, people acting like Jayden's...dead. And I think they will, with him never doing anything wrong before. Why else wouldn't he come home?"

Why else indeed.

"You need to give in and allow a family liaison officer to drop by, though," Helena warned. "His name's Dave Lund, and he's a good source of information and comfort. If we don't find Jayden soon, or if he doesn't return home by himself..." She left it hanging, unable to voice the terrible words.

Katherine blanched. "I can't let myself think that far ahead."

"A few minutes at a time is advisable." Helena smiled, and it felt wrong on her face, despicable and out of place. "I'll ask Dave to call round later, okay? He'll be able to talk you through what we do in situations like this and answer any questions you might have. Shall I say four o'clock?" If she didn't push it, she had a feeling the woman would suffer alone.

Katherine nodded.

"Okay, well, we'll leave you be now, and I'll be in contact as soon as I know anything, all right?"

After she'd collected Jayden's photo from the kitchen, she left Katherine her card, and they walked out, Helena's legs heavy, as well as her heart. In the car, she sighed out her frustration and wished shit like this never happened. Katherine must be going through hell, and she struck Helena as genuine and nothing to do with this. She'd trust her gut on this one. Someone had taken Jayden, for whatever reason, and would hopefully release him tomorrow. Maybe a ransom note would come next. Maybe an explanation would follow after that. Or maybe they'd have to visit Katherine with the awful news that her son wouldn't ever be coming home again.

She blinked back tears and sent Dave an email, letting him know he was needed at Katherine's at four. Once Andy had secured his seat belt, she drove away, down the cliff and into town. At the station, she strode to the front desk.

"Anything?" she asked Louise.

"No, guv. When the phone was pinged, we got nothing. I didn't ask anyone to keep checking it as you didn't say you wanted that."

"I think we ought to have a watch on it, don't you?"

"I'll pass that on."

Helena left her and went upstairs—Andy must have already gone up—and rounded the corner into the incident room. She went straight to the scanner to print off a wad of images of Jayden to be passed around the station so officers knew who they needed to look out for.

Pinning one to the whiteboard, she stared at the boy for a moment, trying to put herself in a mother's shoes. She failed, but it didn't mean she had no empathy. This poor lad, wherever he was, would undoubtedly be petrified.

If he's alive.

She thrust that right out of her head and addressed the team. "What have we got?" She clapped.

Ol jumped and turned her seat to face the room. "Bloody hell, that shit me up, that did."

Helena laughed, feeling guilty for it.

"Let's see," Ol said. "Jayden's got quite a few followers on Instagram. One of the officers talked to Ben Griffin at the school earlier, and he told him Jayden's passwords. They swapped them in case either of them forgot, apparently, so I took it to mean they're seriously best friends if they trust one another like that. I've been able to have a good poke around, and I just got off the phone to the school before you came in. Jayden sent Ben a WhatsApp message at eleven-fifteen this morning."

"What?" Helena's heart thudded, and she rushed over to Ol's desk. "What did it say?"

Ol pulled a face. "It said: *Help me! I'm trapped in the hollow!*"

"What the fuck is this hollow?" Helena said, more to herself than anyone else. It irritated the shit out of her when things weren't clear. "And it confirms the note *is* a part of this now. The poem mentioned a hollow, didn't it. Phil, we should have done this earlier, damn it, but check CCTV outside the station. We'll see whoever posted the note." *Fucking hell, what a missed opportunity.*

"I thought the same about the location in the note," Ol said. "It's so vague. I'm about to do a search now on that to see if there's anything around here called a hollow. It could even be farther afield."

"Okay, you do that." Helena spun and faced Phil. "Did you get a break on the other CCTV?"

He shook his head. "No, although I've checked up on all cars that were heading from the local shops towards the school. I rang the owners, Evan helped, and for now I'd say no one appears to be suspect. I ran checks on them all — none of them have priors, although I think if this is an abduction, someone needs to speak to them in person to get a bead on facial expressions and whatnot. People can easily sound kosher on the phone, can't they, when in reality they're far from it." He gritted his teeth.

"Good idea. Organise that between you," Helena said. "I'm going to the school with Andy to speak to Ben Griffin, although I'll call his mother first and ask her to go down there so she can be present. I don't want my wrist slapped. Someone needs to stay here and keep digging, though, so only two of you go and question the car drivers."

She went to her office and did a search for Mrs Griffin's phone number and placed the call, then rang the school. With the time set for a meeting in twenty minutes in the headmaster's office, Helena grabbed a quick coffee, and then they were off again, driving to Smaltern Secondary.

The high metal gates were locked at the end of the drive, and she had to ring an intercom buzzer on a pole to the right on the pavement. A voice came out of it, surprisingly clear, and Helena introduced them. The gates swung open, and Helena drove through and parked.

In reception, she produced her ID and said she had a meeting with the headmaster.

"I'll just give him a ring now," the young lady behind the desk said, her smile revealing a gap between her two front teeth. She tossed her curly blonde hair over her shoulder while bringing the phone to her ear. "The police are here to see you." She nodded then covered the mouthpiece. "Just go through that door there." She pointed to Helena's left. "His office is the third one on the right."

Helena thanked her and led the way. She knocked on the appropriate door, and Mr Queensley, so his name plaque proclaimed, called them in. Once inside with the door shut, Helena smiled at him and held up her ID. Queensley gestured to four empty chairs in front of his desk, and Helena and Andy sat.

"Ben and his mother will be here in just a moment." Queensley, a broad bloke with a severe receding hairline and ruddy cheeks, shifted his weight a bit and tapped his desk with a finger. "Strange business," he said.

"It is," Helena said, a tad uncomfortable in his presence. Maybe he brought back memories of being at school herself, or perhaps he just gave her the willies in general. *Odd that he called the situation 'strange'. More like disturbing.* "What sort of student would you say Jayden is?"

Queensley blushed. "To be honest, I had to look up his file to see who he is. He's not someone I've had to deal with in the past, and there are so many students here, I can't possibly know them all…"

A piss-poor excuse, but she wouldn't press it.

He grunted. "Ben, on the other hand, acts out a bit in class so…"

A sharp knock at the door had him snapping his mouth shut.

"Come in," he shouted.

A bit unnecessary with the volume, mate?

Helena turned. Ben Griffin was a shock. Tall, brawny, hair cut close to his head, and he looked way older than thirteen. What on earth did he have in common with a lad like Jayden?

She wiped her face of all expression in case her thoughts took it upon themselves to show him what she was thinking. Mother and son sat on the spare seats, Ben with his head down, his mum clasping her hands in her lap. She reminded Helena of a young Goldie Hawn.

Queensley opened his mouth to speak, but Ben got there first.

"It's my fault Jay's gone," he said.

CHAPTER SEVEN

His walk to the police station earlier had given him an ego boost. The Devil had pushed him there, daring him to test the boundaries. Some snotty cow had stared down at him from a high window, and he'd thought about sticking *her* in the tree, and had laughed so hard at that his stomach had hurt.

He was home now, sitting in the drawing room, staring at the scary Jesus. The eyes seemed to bore into him, seeing his thoughts, his secrets, what he really felt about all this. Jesus couldn't find out what he'd done to that kid. He'd never be forgiven and get into Heaven. If he just pretended it was for a good cause, bringing another into the flock, maybe it would be all right. Maybe Jesus would overlook the sin he'd committed.

There wasn't anything he could do to take it back, and he didn't want to most of the time, but two sides of him warred every so often, throwing him into conflicting emotions. The boy he'd been and the man he currently was, argued now and again, and the devil in him added his ten pence worth.

She'd done this, the old bitch. What he had to do next was what *she* had done to him. After the tree. Funny thing was, it would happen in the same house, here, down in the cellar amongst the piles of boxes, the old furniture, cobwebs coating them all, the inhabitants waiting in the middle for flies to land so they could cocoon them, saving them for a later meal.

Down on his knees in front of the scary Jesus, he prayed, asking for guidance, even though Jesus wasn't meant to find out what he was up to. But it had been ingrained in him to do this, so he whispered his pleas that once he'd done to others what had been done to him, this madness, her voice, her appearing as if she wasn't dead, would all go away.

It had to, otherwise he'd go mad.

The answer came, and he rose, got his shoes and coat on, and headed for the hollow. If he gave the kid a clue as to what he was doing there, things would go easier.

He hoped so anyway.

"You can come out now," Grandmother said.

He opened his eyes and jumped. She was right in front of him, the light from the little brass lamp hanging on the inside of the tree glowing on her right cheek. His arms had gone numb, and he'd pissed and shit himself so many times he'd lost count. Where did Mum think he'd been? And how long had he been gone?

He licked his dry lips with an even dryer tongue and wondered if he imagined Grandmother being there. Was he hallucinating through lack of food and water? His stomach was as hollow as the tree, and it had stopped griping hours ago. Or was that days? Time had stretched, and maybe every minute had seemed like an hour. He didn't know; he didn't care. She'd said he could come out, and that was what he'd focus on.

Despite the weird woolly robe, he was freezing, and Grandad's slippers had done nothing to keep his feet warm. She'd allowed him to keep his underpants and socks on, though, but they were damp from wee and —

If he had the energy to blush, he would.

She unlocked the metal clasps around his wrists, and he dropped into a heap, the rough, mossy floor wet with his excretions, his bones jarring — although he had to wonder whether he had any bones, his body was that light and airy. Pain smashed into his armpits from where his arms had been stretched upwards, and he glanced at where he'd been all this time.

A cross had been carved out of the wood, and a picture of the scary Jesus perched on the occasional table, probably taken by Grandmother using her Polaroid, was tacked above it. He shivered, a blast of cold air gusting in through the hole, and then he closed his eyes, hoping for sleep so he wouldn't be in agony anymore.

She gripped his sore, chafed wrists – he tried to scream but failed – and dragged him out, hefting him onto something flat, laying him on it. She must have switched the lamp off in the hollow, as faint light didn't show through his closed eyelids anymore. He wanted to hug himself for warmth but couldn't lift his arms.

Shuffles. Clicks. Snaps. Was she securing the hole?

Then whatever he was on moved, and Grandmother grunted, the sound ominous. He managed to open his eyes. Light came from somewhere, and he reckoned she had the head torch on that she used at night when going out into the garden to put rubbish bags in the bin. She walked in front – lugging him on a sledge? – the rope held over her shoulder. The sledge thing bounced over the woodland floor, and it seemed an age before the ground and his surroundings changed. She pulled him over grass, the sky such a massive and scary *expanse to him in his state of delirium, which crept up on him and threatened to swallow him in one big gulp.*

She stopped and fiddled with something up ahead, and he guessed it to be her rear garden gate that backed onto the cliff top. A creak of the ring handle turning, then she tugged the rope, taking him into the confines of her high fencing.

Relief slapped at him — he was safe…or as safe as he could be with a raving lunatic grandparent. He flaked out, everything too much, and hoped he'd never wake up again.

Jayden's stomach cramped. He was so hungry, and he'd lost count of how long he'd been there. Everywhere hurt — he'd swear even his hair did, his teeth — and he'd lost the ability to cry tears a while ago. His eyes were as dry as his mouth. What time was it? Mum would be going crazy by now, worrying about him, thinking he'd run away, or worse, that he was dead. Even if he'd only been gone for a few hours, she'd know something had happened. He'd never been late home from school in his life — well, not past five o'clock anyway, unless she knew he was going to Ben's for tea.

Was that what she'd thought when he hadn't shown up? Maybe she'd given it a while, waiting for him, then had tried calling him. Had his phone rung in the park, the tune mournful beneath the slide? Did it even work since he'd dropped it? Or had Balaclava picked it up without Jayden noticing?

Maybe someone else had found it and would get hold of Mum or Ben.

He could only hope.

He shivered, so cold he couldn't feel his hands and feet, his legs and arms slowly going the same way. He didn't want to wet himself again—it had taken ages for him to shake off the tremors from the dampness of his skin.

Struggling but determined, Jayden wiggled his fingers until the string pull landed on his palm—he only knew it had by the weight on the end pressing it into his hand. He curled stiff fingers and tugged, but it was useless. He must have spent about an hour—or so he thought—battling to get the light on, and he succeeded at last, squinting at the little brass lamp, absurdly wondering where it had come from. It was old, like something a granny owned.

He turned his head to stare ahead, and pain shot up his neck.

The note on the wall had been changed: *Repent, and all will be well.*

He blinked, slowly, processing the words, processing the fact that Balaclava must have been back to have switched it over with the message about the light. Why hadn't Jayden woken up? Had Balaclava done anything to him while he'd been out of it?

He shuddered, the action bringing on a fresh load of pain, and he just about managed to tug the lamp off, then blacked out right along with it.

CHAPTER EIGHT

"What do you mean, Ben?" Queensley asked, puffing his chest out.

Helena had been about to ask the same thing.

"If we hadn't rowed, this wouldn't have happened," Ben said.

Oh. Well. Tell us something we don't know.

Helena was narked, deflated by his words. She'd thought Ben was going to give them something else, but he was just blaming himself, nothing more. So she didn't say something inappropriate, she raised her eyebrows at Queensley, hoping he'd speak instead.

"A boy doesn't go missing just because you had a spat," Queensley said. "Now, show the police officers that message from Jamie."

"Jayden," Helena supplied, further annoyed.

"Yes, Jayden. Quite." Queensley pushed out a long breath, ruffling papers on his desk, perhaps to hide his embarrassment.

Ben got his phone out, found the WhatsApp message, and passed the mobile to Helena.

"We'll have to take this," she said. "Jayden may contact you again, and we need to be right on it if he does. This way, we'll know when his phone is on, then we can ping it and find his location closest to the nearest tower."

Ben opened his mouth, probably to protest, but Goldie Hawn put a hand on his knee, squeezing — a bit too forcefully, Helena reckoned — and he remained quiet.

"We're not interested in anything on your phone other than your messages from Jayden, okay?" Helena hoped she sounded reassuring, but it wouldn't do the kid any harm not to have a gadget propped up in front of his face for a day or so. And, yes, they would be nosing through his phone, but for this investigation, unless he was implicated in Jayden's disappearance or there was evidence of a serious crime, she wouldn't do anything with the information. "Do you need a PIN to access it?"

Goldie shook her head. "I don't allow that, not until he's eighteen."

Helena didn't know how she felt about that. Ben might only be a teenager, but he still needed privacy. Anyway, that was Goldie's affair, and Helena couldn't allow herself to get caught up in the pros and cons of it.

She slid the phone in her pocket and would put it in an evidence bag once they got back to the car. "Do you know what Jayden means by 'the hollow', Ben?"

He shook his head. "No idea. I've been trying to think, but...nothing."

"Can you tell me what your little argument was about?"

He blushed and kicked at the cheap, wiry grey carpet with one shoe. "Do I have to?" He looked excruciatingly uncomfortable.

"Would you prefer to write it down for me?"

He nodded. Queensley tutted and handed over a piece of paper and a pen. The lad got up and walked over to a filing cabinet so no one could see what he was writing—mainly his mother, Helena suspected.

"I really don't see why he can't just say," Goldie piped up.

Shame you're not as pleasant as the real Goldie Hawn.

Although Helena didn't have kids, she remembered being a teen well. Small things to adults were big things to a child, and although Helena might shrug off what he showed her as no big deal, to Ben, it might be everything. "Teenagers have just as much right to privacy as

70

anyone else, Mrs Griffin. If Ben prefers to put it on paper, that's fine by me. So long as I get the info I want, it doesn't matter how he delivers it."

"Well, I disagree. He's underage. What he gets up to is my business."

"To a degree." Helena stopped right there. She wasn't going to get into a slanging match and have the woman ask her if she had children, and with Helena's answer, she could smugly tell her to shut her mouth because she couldn't possibly know what she was talking about. Helena didn't need to have kids to know this lad probably had a stifled home life where every move was watched and poked into.

Which put him firmly out of the picture with regards to Jayden's disappearance in her opinion. Ben probably couldn't move without being spotted or questioned, so how would he pull off an abduction? And he was a minor — would he have it in him to do this? No, she didn't think he did.

Ben coughed, and Helena turned to look at him. He held the paper out, so she got up, raising a hand at Goldie when she made a move to rise as well. Helena took the paper from him and read it.

I like this girl and was going to ask her out. Jayden laughed at what I was going to say to her, said it was cheesy, like something my dad would say, and it upset me. I don't have a dad. He left when I was a baby. So it pissed me off. Jayden thinks my dad works away on an oil rig because that's what I told him. I walked off and stuck my finger up at him, and that was the last time I saw him.

Helena folded the paper and slipped it into her pocket so there was no chance of Goldie getting hold of it. "Thank you." She patted his arm and gestured for him to take a seat.

He slumped down beside his mother. Her face was red, eyes narrowed, and she was so clearly annoyed she had no sway in what was going on here. He'd be in for a grilling later, no doubt about it.

Helena sat. "Ben, where did you last see Jayden?"

"In the playground. There were other kids about if you don't believe me. They'd have seen."

"I believe you, don't worry about that. I'm asking so I get a picture of what happened, okay, not because I don't trust what you're saying. So all my next questions are based on that, all right? We need to work out where Jayden went, see?"

He nodded, his shoulders slumping where the tension of accusation slid off them.

"Where did you go after you last spoke to him?" She didn't want to mention him giving

72

the rude hand gesture. God knew what Goldie would say about that.

"I walked the usual route home." He explained where that was. "I got in about four, I think."

"It was twelve minutes past four," Goldie said.

Bloody hell. A clock-watcher as well as a nosy bint. Poor kid.

Helena ignored the woman. "Did you see Jayden on that walk home?"

"No. I turned around to see if he was following, but he wasn't there. I ended up walking with Shona Long."

"Shona?" Goldie gave him a critical stare. "*I* don't know any Shona."

"She's my mate's girlfriend," Ben said in exasperation.

"Less of the tone, young man," Goldie snapped.

Well, a domestic between a mother and her son wasn't what Helena needed. "Mrs Griffin, can you please remain quiet during this interview — unless you have any information we need to know regarding Jayden?" She lifted her eyebrows to hammer home her point — butt the fuck out.

"Only that I can't see him going off like this," Goldie said. "From the times he's been at ours for tea, I'd say he's a polite and lovely child and not prone to being stroppy with his mother."

A public dig at her son. What a mean woman.

Ben toed the carpet again and folded his hands in his lap. Helena would put money down on him moving out of the family home as soon as he was able. She'd been brought up in a liberal household where, by Ben's age, she'd been afforded the same respect as an adult. Ben's situation hurt her heart. It must be terribly difficult to live where he was so stifled.

"Ben, did you walk the whole way home with Shona?" Helena asked.

"Yeah. She lives in our street. We were seen — she spoke to Clara when we waited to cross Norby Road."

Helena glanced at Andy — he was writing in his notebook.

"Okay. Why didn't you answer Jayden's message when he said he was sorry?" She knew the answer but needed to check all the same.

"I was still annoyed. I was going to WhatsApp him last night but forgot. So I thought of doing it today, but he didn't turn up for school, and then I got that other message when I was in maths…" He slapped himself on the head.

"Stop that," Goldie said. "It makes you look strange."

Queensley growled, Andy coughed, and Ben flushed scarlet. The tension in the air was rife. Helena glared at Goldie for a few seconds until the harridan gave up the battle and conceded defeat, staring down at her feet.

"Ben, are you sure you don't know what the hollow is?" Helena asked.

He turned to look at her. "I swear, I haven't got a clue what he's on about. There's no hollow around here, is there? It could be anything. A ditch? What?" He raised his hands then dropped them to his sides. "I can't think of anything. I'd tell you if I knew. He's my mate." His face crumpled a little.

So she didn't force him to endure the humiliation of crying and his mother telling him off for *that*, too, she stood. "Thank you, Ben, you've been a massive help, I promise. Don't worry about anything, okay? We'll get your phone back to you as soon as we can, and whatever is on there is *your* business, all right?"

She doubted he'd dare have anything bad on there anyway, not when Hawn the Hawk probably poked through it at her leisure. Anger threatened to come to the boil, so Helena walked to the door and opened it.

Goldie stood and flapped a hand impatiently at Ben for him to do the same. They left the room, and Helena closed the door, that lad very much on her mind. If anything happened to

Jayden, Ben would beat himself up for life, she reckoned.

"Well, this really is a terrible situation," Queensley said.

Helena retook her seat. "It is. Can you get this Shona Long's phone number for me—well, her mother's? I need to give her a ring to see if she'd rather be here when I question her daughter."

Queensley tapped on his keyboard, seeming chuffed he had an important role here today. Helena inwardly cringed at how someone could feel happy in a situation like this.

Weirdo.

"Here you go," he said, jotting it down on a small pad.

Helena leant over and typed one set of digits into her phone—she'd chosen the mother's mobile. "Hi, is this Shona Long's mum?"

"Yes, this is Christine."

"This is DI Helena Stratton—there's absolutely nothing to worry about, so don't panic. I'm at the school and need to speak to Shona to confirm she walked home with Ben Griffin and—"

"She did. I saw them out of the window."

"Nevertheless, I still need to confirm it with her. Do you want to come down here as her appropriate adult, or is it okay that Mr Queensley is present?"

"I'm at work and can't get out—I'm with a client—so it's fine. Go ahead and chat to her."

"Thank you. It really is only to make sure she walked home with him and whether she saw Jayden Rook at any point."

"Why, what's happened?" A tinge of fear crept into Christine's voice.

"I'm afraid Jayden didn't arrive home from school yesterday." It would probably be leaked to the bloody news soon enough, so Mrs Long would find out anyway, but at the same time, Helena felt she had to be open with her when it was her daughter she'd be questioning.

"Oh God! That's awful. Is there anything I can do? I know Jayden's mum."

"Maybe call round there when you have time? She's refusing to see anyone apart from our family liaison officer, though, so be prepared to get knocked back at the door." *In other words, respect her wishes.*

"I'll go there at lunchtime—I can take the afternoon off. Christ, poor woman. This is heartless of me, and I don't mean to come off like that, but I really do have to go…"

"I understand."

While Queensley rang reception to ask for Shona to come to the office, they sat in silence. Helena passed Ben's note to Andy to bring him up to speed. He read it and handed it back, eyes narrowed.

Finally, Shona arrived and, although she appeared to be shitting bricks, she confirmed what Ben had said, her voice shaking. They'd walked home together, hadn't seen Jayden, and had stopped for a moment to talk to a Clara on Norby Road. CCTV would confirm that as Norby was a main thoroughfare and traffic cams were in place, but still, Helena didn't think these kids were involved.

Now it was time to get to it and find out who was.

CHAPTER NINE

In the lemon glow of the brass lamp, the cold chomped at Jayden—so cold now he guessed nighttime might be here. His chest constricted, and he panicked at not having his inhaler. It had been in his blazer pocket, and he guessed Balaclava must have taken his uniform with him, because it wasn't in the tree. Not that he'd be able to get to it anyway with his hands being held up like they were.

He did that thing the asthma nurse had told him to do when he got anxious. Ground himself, pick five things he could see, four to feel, three to hear, two for smell, one for taste.

See: The roughly hewn tree walls covered in moss. The message about repenting. The hook the other torch had hung on. The tartan slippers. The red stuff on his palms.

Feel: Anger, fear, vulnerability, bewilderment. If he could actually *feel* something, touch it, he'd have chosen just one. Mum's cheek on the top of his head.

Hear: His laboured breathing. Him wheezing. His chest whistling.

Smell: Piss. Earth. He could go on...mulch, sweat, his rancid breath.

Taste: Terror.

All of it focused on his situation, so he wasn't any calmer. He'd try the 'grounding chair' technique, where he sat somewhere comfortable, his feet flat on the floor, breathing in then out for the count of three, concentrating on his body, not what was in his head, but he didn't have a fucking chair, did he. He could hold on to something and pin all his attention on it, but he couldn't grasp the string pull or the metal ball on the end of it. And as for distracting himself... What with?

Panic welled up, his chest tightening, and he knew he wasn't going to get out of this without having an asthma attack. He could let it come, do what it always did, and hope it would pass, but something told him it wouldn't this time, which created a higher level of apprehension. The more he tried to think of something else, the more his circumstances filled his mind.

This wasn't going to turn out to his advantage.

The knowledge that death loomed was a real possibility. His head lightened, and he tried to suck air in to fill his lungs, but they weren't opening up enough to let any inside.

He closed his eyes, the last thing in his head his mum, smiling at him, telling him everything was going to be okay.

"Everything's going to be okay," Katherine whispered, staring out into the front garden at Dave Lund walking down the path to his car, the streetlamp casting him in an amber shroud.

He'd been with her for three hours, and she'd assured him she'd be fine on her own now. Before he'd arrived, Christine Long had turned up and, although Katherine had wanted to scream at her to fuck off, she'd let her in for the length of time it had taken to make, then drink, a cuppa.

Was it really that time already? A whole twenty-seven hours that Jayden had been gone? She still had yesterday's clothes on, but how could she go off and have a bath or a shower, do normal things, when her baby was God knew where? No, if he was suffering, so would she.

He'd come back, wouldn't he? Dave had assured her that Helena and Andy were the best people to have on the case, along with three others who did all the checking at the station. She couldn't remember their names, but he'd written them down for her, along with their numbers, so she could ring them if she wanted. The thing was, she didn't want to. In the past, she'd imagined how she'd feel if this sort of thing ever happened to her—and it was always someone else who had to go through this, it would never be her; what a stupid bitch she was to have been so naïve—and she'd told herself she'd be on the police's case twenty-four seven, except…she wasn't. If she didn't ring them, she wouldn't be reminded Jayden wasn't there.

Oh, she knew he wasn't, of course she did, but a small part of her pretended he'd just gone to stay with someone for a while and she'd see him again soon.

If she didn't think along those lines, she'd go mad.

He couldn't help himself. Compelled to visit the boy again to make sure he was okay, he stood outside the tree with Grandmother's head torch on. He'd convinced himself on the walk there that he was doing the right thing—more than Grandmother had done for him.

She stood next to him now, pecking words out through her spiteful beak, nudging him in the side with a fleshy elbow. "This goes against the teachings. If he knows you're checking on him, he won't be as scared or feel so alone. The idea is for him to be so frightened, that by the time you get him out, he'll be pliable."

Pliable? That must have been how she'd seen him, someone easily manipulated, and he'd fallen straight into her trap. Fear did that to you, good and proper.

"Stop speaking to me," he said, his skin hot beneath the balaclava. "In fact, stop fucking appearing and all."

"Language…" She tutted.

Sod the language. She needed to know it was *his* time now—he was in control, not her. She'd relinquished that right the day she'd taken her last breath.

Are you in control, though? Or is it still her? It is, isn't it…

"Bugger off," he said—to that sneaky little voice in his head and to her.

She harrumphed and glided off, into the trees and out of sight.

Sort yourself out. Remember why you're here.

If he just peeked in, ensured the lad was okay, he could go home and sleep in peace—

providing Grandmother didn't pop up and perch her massive arse on the side of his bed, settling in for a chat.

More like a preach.

Tomorrow afternoon, once darkness came, he'd get Jayden out and give him the speech, then send him home, assured in the knowledge the words he whispered to him would mean Jayden wouldn't blab about where he'd been or what had happened to him. He'd want to seek the Lord and go to church. He'd be a good boy, too scared to do otherwise. Father Pinto would welcome him into his arms and show him the light, and he could join the choir.

Nodding to himself, he released the padlocks on the tree, slipping the bunch of keys into his pocket. He had a Thermos with him, containing chicken soup, and if Jayden agreed right now to come into the flock, he might find himself drinking it in a minute. If he didn't…well, he'd get nothing. He could starve.

He curled his index fingers around two of the metal arches and pulled. The circle came out easily now he'd sanded the moss down. He placed it beside the tree, surprised the lamp was on inside, despite him leaving a note to warn the boy to be sensible in using it. He stepped in, his gaze going straight to the picture of the scary Jesus above Jayden's head, one he'd nailed there, not the Polaroid that had been ruined by damp in the years since he'd been held prisoner.

No, not a prisoner. Never that. A disciple.

"That's right," Grandmother said, appearing beside him again.

The space was cramped with them all in there, so he pushed her out into the woods and stood in front of the hole, blocking her from getting back in.

Jayden was just like the real Jesus, hanging on the cross, his palms bleeding, although he was sure Jesus hadn't worn slippers. He'd wanted to recreate his own scene here as closely as possible through fear the lesson might not work if things were different. Yet here he was, breaking the rules anyway, visiting the lad.

The boy's skin was a bit grey, his lips purple, scabs dried out where he'd punched him, the surrounding area blue. Dried blood streaked his face from where his nose had bled. Perhaps this winter was colder than the one he'd endured, and that was why he looked so freezing.

Moving forward, he prodded Jayden in the chest and held his breath, waiting for him to wake up and see him standing there, much like what had happened when Grandmother had told him he could leave the hollow. But Jayden remained asleep. Had he died like Jesus? Would he come to life again at Easter if he put him in a cave down by the shore, blocking him inside with rocks?

Confused, he shook the boy—hard—but Jayden still didn't stir.

He stepped up close, placing his ear in front of Jayden's nose.

No air came out. No sound of him breathing in sleep.

Panicked, he pressed a hand to the cold chest, and it didn't rise and fall like it should. Christ, was Jayden *really* dead? Worried beyond belief, he scrabbled in his pocket for the keys and unlocked the metal cuffs. Jayden fell down onto his side, and the similarity to the past incited chills that rippled all over him. This wasn't supposed to happen. He didn't want to *kill* anyone, just teach them the Lord's way.

"Fuck..." he said, his head torch lighting the body in all its stark glory. "Christ, oh Lord, please tell me what to do."

"I thought you weren't telling Jesus about this?" Grandmother sniped from outside. "If you want my advice, you need to get rid of him."

Her imperious tone nearly sent him over the edge into full-blown terror. His heart raced too quickly, and he took deep breaths to calm himself. All he'd wanted was to expand the flock, not take away from it.

"Oh God..."

"He won't want anything to do with this," Grandmother said, poking him in the back. "Don't drag Him into this mess, which, I might add, you created."

"*You* did this," he said, believing it. "If you hadn't brainwashed me…"

"I can't have. If you were brainwashed, you wouldn't even think I'd done such a thing." Her huff of grey cloudy breath sailed over his shoulder and into the hollow, loitering there for a moment then dissipating.

She was right, the good side of him conceded that point, but one of the other sides, the one infused by the Devil… He drew on that, on the evilness it wrought in him, and, just like Grandmother had done to him, he dragged Jayden out of the tree. There was no sledge—he'd planned to use that tomorrow—so he'd have to lift the body and sling it over his shoulder the same as he'd done when he'd first taken Jayden. Now, though, he needed to secure the hollow. He dumped Jayden on the ground then went inside to switch off the lamp. Securing the circle door in place, he then returned to the lifeless kid, picked him up, and walked towards the park. It took ages, and his shoulders ached, but he plodded on, the torch beam bobbing with each step.

Finally, he reached the tree line and doused the head torch. Sometimes, kids came there at night to sit around on the wooden benches, and he didn't need anyone seeing him. From what he could gather, no one was about, so he placed Jayden on the ground beneath the slide awning and removed the slippers and robe.

Then he took Jayden's phone out, replaced the SIM and battery, and switched it on. There was nothing he could say that would fix this, other than that he was sorry and it hadn't been his intention for Jayden to die, but he didn't dare risk writing a long message. A short one would have to do.

He turned the mobile off, wiped it all over with the robe to remove his prints, and placed it beside the body. The boy looked pitiful there in just his underpants and socks, but again, that wasn't his fault.

How was he to know the kid would snuff it?

CHAPTER TEN

*H*elena stared at Uthway, who'd hauled her to her feet and now walked around her, inspecting his 'goods'. She shivered at his perusal, thinking of what was going through his mind. She'd told him she was too old to be auctioned off, but he'd said some men preferred women of her age, especially ones with such lovely long hair like hers.

She couldn't wait for the moment she'd get it all cut off.

"You're not bad actually," he said, coming to stand in front of her.

His eyes…God, they frightened her, so 'seeing', so able to spot her weaknesses. She'd been trained for certain scenarios, and whatever she'd learnt had deserted her since she'd been brought to this crappy metal storage container high on the cliffs. His treatment of her — his sidekick's, too — had rendered her pliant and malleable, although he didn't know how she felt inside. Outwardly, she was doing as he told her, but in her heart and mind? Fuck, she was just waiting for a chance to escape.

She would not be sold.

A wicked part of her mind whispered otherwise from time to time, and although she'd all but given up hope a few hours ago when they'd 'tested' her body to see whether it would be 'roadworthy' as Uthway had put it, now she'd had time to think, she couldn't give up. She had to get out of there to save the other women — but that might have already been done. Her colleagues knew the location of the holding house — Lime Street — and while Helena was holed up in here, maybe those people had been saved.

"You could pass for mid-twenties," Uthway went on. "No stretch marks — always a bonus. And you're tight."

She hid a wince. His way of putting things was revolting.

"Yeah, I think you'll do, but I reckon I need yet one more go before I properly make up my mind."

Oh Christ, no…

He roughly pulled her out of the corner and pushed her back onto the floor, and she endured what he did to her, thinking not of what was happening but of Emilija, the Lithuanian woman who'd escaped Lime Street a few hours before Uthway's thug had dragged Helena into a white van and brought her

90

here. She thought of her life if she didn't break free, and she thought of the man waiting for her in the future, willing to pay a hefty price to have a sex bride locked in a room, there for wherever he wanted to take her. Those images and the fear for what was to come was better than acknowledging Uthway pawing at her.

Mercifully, it was over quickly, and she had the mad urge to make a jibe on how long he'd lasted but decided she'd better not. He'd get arsey, slap her about, and she needed a clear head, not a bruised and cloudy one.

Uthway got off her and zipped up his jeans. Staring down at her, he said, "See, you even look like a proper slave. You're just splayed there, legs open and all that. You'll take to it well. Good girl."

Condescending bastard.

He left her then, locking her inside, the darkness creeping in around her. She'd never get used to it, never sleep without the light on again, providing she got out of here. Providing her new 'master' let her keep a lamp on.

No, she wouldn't think that way. She'd be back in her own bed in no time.

That was what kept her going.

Home.

"Did you hear anything I just said?" Zach raised his eyebrows, staring at her from across the table in Mustak Cuisine.

Helena jolted out of her head, a blush flooding her cheeks. The low Indian music playing in the background flowed into her ears. "So sorry. I get like that sometimes, you know I do. Drifting off. It wasn't you, I promise."

"I was going to ask if my conversation skills were lacking again." He winked and lifted his glass of lemonade, taking a long sip.

She laughed. "No, I just… Images came back, that's all."

"Ah, I'm sorry to hear that."

And she knew he was. This year, he'd shown her what being with a man *should* be like—he was caring, attentive, giving her time to breathe. They didn't see each other that often, maybe three nights a week, but it was enough, especially since she didn't quite have it in her yet to fall headlong into anything more serious, not after the crap she'd put up with from Marshall.

He was in prison now, his trial next month, and God, she was glad he'd become an ex before she'd found out he was a warped son of a bitch who'd gone round killing three sisters. That would have put the proverbial cat amongst the pigeons if they'd still been an item. As it was, she'd endured questioning from Yarworth about a month after the case, asking her if she'd picked up on anything sinister when she'd been seeing Marshall. She'd been cleared of any involvement, obviously, but still, the idea that Yarworth had hinted she'd known what Marshall was capable of had rankled.

Yet another reason to think the chief was a twat.

"You've done it again," Zach said. "Shall we skip dessert and call it a night?"

"Christ. Sorry. I don't know what's going on with me this evening. Tired probably."

"Got a heavy workload?" he asked.

She sat back and stared at the remnants of her meal—a chicken korma and tri-colour pilau rice, a wedge of naan bread hanging off the side of her plate—and nodded. "A missing lad."

"Oh…"

"Plus, some weirdo sent a poison pen letter— the old-fashioned kind. If that's to be believed, the kid will be released tomorrow—if the note is even anything to do with him."

"What, they cut letters out and everything?" Zach's frown was so deep his eyebrows met in the middle.

"Yep, and delivered it by hand to the station. Is that brazen or what? The CCTV outside caught them on camera, and I say 'them' because they had a hoodie on, pulled low over their face, and a bomber-type jacket bulked them out. And it was dark, so we can't tell if it's a man or woman. Mind you, I'm leaning towards a man because of the build." She thought about

93

the Landon case and how they'd thought they'd been looking for a female killer, when, in fact, it had been a man in disguise—using a mask and a blonde wig.

"Bloody hell," Zach said, rubbing his forehead, smoothing out the furrows.

Helena's phone rang, inappropriate bastard that it was, and she sighed, pulling it out of her inside jacket pocket. It was the front desk, so she swiped to receive the call.

"It's Clive, guv."

What was he doing working behind the desk? He was a PC who spent most of his time out in the field. He'd come back to work ten months ago after being stabbed by Landon, the one who'd worn the mask, and thankfully seemed none the worse for wear.

"What can I do for you?" she asked.

"Jayden Rook's phone has been switched on, and Ben Griffin's chirped up with a message from it. I've been keeping an eye on them all evening—Louise left me a note about it."

She shot upright and leant her elbows on the table, clutching the phone tight. "When?"

"About half an hour ago."

"What was the message?" She willed it to be something they could use and not another mention of that bloody hollow.

"It said: *I'm in the park. Sorry.*"

"Okay, what about the phone now? On or off?"

"We've been able to locate it, and it's in the park."

"Okay, have you sent an officer down there?"

"Yes, guv, I sent two. I would have gone myself, but I'm needed on the desk. The usual night sergeant called in sick, so I'm pulling a double until Louise can take over after having a bit of kip."

"Right. So have they collected the phone?"

"Yes, but there's something else there and all."

"Like what?"

Clive took a deep breath—it sounded weary. "A body."

"Shit." She'd said that a little too loudly.

People from other tables glanced over, some laughing, some frowning in disapproval.

"Give me a second, Clive. I'm in Mustak."

She gestured to Zach to pay the bill—she'd give him her half later—then went outside, the chill immediately encompassing her, and she leant against the wall, the bricks cold on her arse and back.

"How old is the body?" she asked. "I mean the age, not how long they've been dead."

"Um, it seems to be Jayden."

Freezing dread steeped in her stomach, and her legs weakened. Adrenaline whipped through her, and she closed her eyes to stop the world spinning. "Fuck it."

"My thought exactly. It's the main park in the centre of town. He's under the slide."

The image that conjured had Helena wanting to cry. He was just thirteen, for God's sake. "Don't inform the mother yet. Leave that to me."

"I wasn't going to, guv."

"Sorry, I know you wouldn't. I just…I want to make sure it's him first, that's all. She's going through enough as it is." She glanced to the left at Mustak's door opening. "Zach's here with me, so we'll go down now. Get on to SOCO."

"They're already en route. I got hold of them before you. Thought it would be best to get a tent up as soon as possible because of the location. Some kids came along to drink cider on the bloody benches, but hopefully they've gone now."

"Actually, it would be handy if they were still there. They might have seen something. Never mind. Speak soon."

She walked with Zach to his car, her heart thumping hard. She didn't tell him anything until they'd got inside, their seat belts secured.

"Fucking hell," he said. "Not good."

"You're telling me."

"I actually thought you were going to find him alive."

96

"Hmm. This is absolutely horrible. His poor mother. I dread to think what he must have gone through."

Zach drove off, and Helena pondered on why anyone would want to kill a child. It wasn't something a sane person would even contemplate, so they had to be looking for someone who didn't have a damn conscience or was mentally unstable. If the family had no murk in their pasts, why on earth had Jayden been picked? Was it random like she'd thought before? And what was the fucking point of it?

"We're here," Zach said.

Blimey, she hadn't even noticed until he'd said. She got out and waited for Zach to take his bag out of the boot. While she was at it, she pinched a white outfit, booties, and gloves, and got dressed in the car park. Zach did the same, then together they walked towards the play area. Half of it had been cordoned off with tape, and a tent had been erected over the slide, quite a big one so it covered the whole thing and the surrounding safety flooring. On the other side, the kids Clive had mentioned loitered about, lifting two-litre plastic cider bottles to their mouths or smoking fags.

She called out to them. "I'm not interested in the fact you're clearly underage and drinking, but I need to speak to you for a minute, all right?" She pointed at the tent. "About that."

"Yeah," one of them said, lowering his bottle then taking a drag of his cigarette, as though even if she did reprimand them about their bad habits, he didn't give a toss.

She counted five of them — three lads and two girls — and made her way over, sending Andy a quick message for him to get down here as soon as he could, unless he preferred for her to deal with it. Standing in front of the kids, their faces shadowy in the darkness — the light from inside the tent didn't reach that far — she said, "What time did you arrive here?"

"After the coppers," a boy said, brown hair, looked fifteen but could be younger. A cigarette dangled from the corner of his mouth.

"So you didn't see anyone else in here?" Helena asked.

"No. Just that pair." He jerked his thumb at two uniforms standing by the tape and took a drag of his fag.

Helena was getting annoyed at his nonchalance. "Did you see anyone on your way in here?"

"No." A girl, dark hair.

Helena sighed. "Anyone outside the park, as if they'd been in here?"

The other two lads wandered off about three metres away to sit on a bench.

"No." The boy again. He swigged some cider, the plastic crackling where the bottle was half empty.

"That'll pickle your liver," Helena said.

"There's someone under the slide." He nodded in that direction. "Saw the feet poking out. Then they came with the tent. That's a dead body when they use a tent." He looked her up and down. "And you're wearing them clothes. *A Touch of Frost* or what. My nan watches that on DVD."

"Is it Jayden?" the other girl asked.

It was then Helena recognised Shona Long. *Shit.* "I have no idea. Best you go home, eh? It's cold, and you shouldn't be here when this sort of thing is going on."

She waited for the five of them to trudge away, to leave the park by the main black-painted iron gates, then she walked over to the tent. A deep breath in, and she opened the flap.

The lights seemed brighter than usual, but maybe that was because she'd got used to the dark outside. There was quite a bit of ground space between her and the actual slide, and several SOCOs were on hands and knees, looking for evidence. Zach was beneath a log cover that hung in a bottomless triangle over bench seats beneath the silver slide, and with him was a body. Socks...white socks covered the feet, one of them pulled off slightly so the toe

99

part flopped. Had that happened when the abductor had taken the shoes off?

Christ.

Boxer shorts, the only other piece of clothing, gave the kid some dignity, but God only knew whether he'd had any prior to death. His slender body had been placed on its back, legs together, straight, the arms pushed to his sides. Helena took another breath, sighed it out, then plodded over there. She stared down at the blood-streaked face—yes, it was Jayden.

"I've taken his temp via the ear," Zach said, "and although the cold weather usually buggers things up, I think this lad died within the hour, maybe two."

So recent. While they'd been enjoying their dinner.

Hers wanted to come back up.

"Any obvious signs as yet?" She was asking a bit much, considering they'd only just got here.

"Not from my quick glance. He has no bruising, although I haven't looked at his back yet, but as you can see, he was maybe in a punch-up. A row with someone after school? Was he being bullied and hadn't told anyone?"

Helena stared at Jayden's lips. Scabs had formed over where they'd been split, so time had passed between him getting smacked in the mouth and now. Dried blood sat in his nostrils.

A punch to the nose? Zach pushed the lad onto his side.

"Nothing here. Oh, hang on." He peered closer. "He's hit his head on something. There's a small gash. His hair's matted with dried blood."

"Is the gash big enough to indicate he died from a blow to the skull?"

"There's a bit of a bump—half an egg—so it seems he took quite a wallop. Doesn't appear to be your usual trauma with a blunt object of the weapon variety, but I'll know more when I do the PM. Can't say for definite whether he was whacked by someone or fell and hit it. No strangulation marks, although there is some redness to the skin beneath the eyes." He lowered the body, removed the smeared glasses, and held them up.

Helena took an evidence bag out of Zach's medical holdall, and he popped the specs inside. The sight of them was heartbreaking, and she handed them to a SOCO.

Zach opened one of Jayden's eyes. "Pronounced veins on the whites. Could have been suffocated with something held over his nose and mouth, although there's no bruising from the force that would be needed to hold the head in place—no fingertip marks. Red eyelid rims. Speckles of petechiae on the upper cheeks—trouble breathing or maybe caused by coughing. I need to get a look at his lungs to know what went on in that regard. Want me to check for sexual abuse now or tomorrow?"

"Now." She turned away.

Andy walked in, suited and booted, his face wreathed in a grim expression. "Is it...?"

She nodded. "Matches the picture we have of him."

"Fuck." He stared up at the roof of the tent, then back to her. "We'll need to go and see Katherine sooner rather than later."

"We will." She told him about the message from Jayden's phone to Ben's. "Bloody good job we took it off him. Can you imagine him coming down here when he got the message and finding his mate like this?"

"He'd be scarred for life." Andy shook his head. "Any cause of death yet?"

"Possibly difficulty breathing."

"Suffocation?"

"Looks likely." The idea of Jayden having a pillow pressed over his face brought on nausea. She swallowed.

"Look at his wrists and palms," Andy said.

Helena didn't. She couldn't face seeing what Zach was doing to the boy. "Tell me instead."

"He's been cuffed I'm willing to bet; the skin's red raw, circular marks. Looks like there's blood on his palms."

"No sign of anything sexual here," Zach called out.

Thank God. "Okay. What's that on his hands?" She faced him.

"Seems to be red paint. It's like stigmata. A religious angle maybe?"

"It's possible. We'll look into it. Um, we're going to have to visit the mother. I'll give you a call in the morning."

"All right. Sweet dreams." Zach smiled and got on with his work.

She wouldn't be having sweet dreams after this. More like a sodding nightmare.

CHAPTER ELEVEN

By the light of a full moon, he watched three kids fucking about on the cliff top, alcohol of some description in a boy's hand, as well as a lit cigarette. These children had seriously forsaken God and needed bringing into the fold, but he couldn't take them all, so maybe a good talking to would help.

They approached him, laughing and jeering, so he stared out at the sea as though their presence didn't intimidate him. That was the key with the youth of today — don't show fear. The minute you did, they'd be on you.

"What are you doing up here on your own, you weirdo?" a skinny lad said, cracking up at his crappy conversation starter, bravado probably brought on by the cheap booze.

"Thinking about God," he said, "and how knowing him and Jesus enriches my life." *Convincing myself that's still the case. Hearing lots of voices in my head that confuse me.*

A few chuckles sailed along, quickly swallowed by the *shush* and *whoosh* of the waves. He turned to get a better look at the kids. They were teens, just the right age, the boy and two girls. One girl stared at him as though he was mad, so he gazed back kindly and smiled.

"Do you pray?" he asked her.

She shrugged. Obviously didn't want to give an honest answer in front of her friends. Did she think it would make her look stupid? But everyone prayed at some point in their lives, didn't they, whether they were believers in God or not. Everyone asked for guidance. *Please let that boy fancy me. Please let Mum buy me those new jeans. Please make it sunny tomorrow so my hair doesn't get ruined in the rain.* All meaningless requests. Self-serving.

"What about you?" he asked the boy.

"Fuck that."

"Don't be rude, Stephan," the second girl said.

At least one of them had some manners.

"Just give it a try," he said. "Stand here in a line and close your eyes. Ask God for whatever you want."

Stephan giggled uneasily. "God doesn't exist."

"That's because you're not allowing him to," he said. "Your mind is closed off to the possibility. Mine was once, but look at me now. I'm devout. A true believer." *Most of the time.*

"Let's just do it." Girl number one. "Can't do any harm, can it? Then we can go and find somewhere warm, because I've had enough. It's bloody freezing out here."

"That's because you didn't drink any of this," Stephan said, holding up a plastic bottle of cider with about an inch of fluid left in the bottom. "It heats you up. I'm toasty."

They stood in a row facing the sea, those three kids, lambs to the slaughter, and when they'd closed their eyes, their chatter silenced for a moment until Stephan giggled again. Their positions were girl, girl, boy. He listened to what the voices told him to do, and the Devil piped up the loudest, so he moved back several paces behind the girls and raised his hands, ran at them, stopped short, then shoved them both in the back at the same time. Hard. Two shrieks, then they were falling, those shrieks turning to screams and Stephan shouting, "Oh my God, oh my God...what the actual *fuck*?"

The cider bottle followed the girls over, Stephan losing his grip on it.

"Language," he said, hating himself for it. He wasn't like Grandmother. He was different.

"How the hell did they fall?" Stephan asked, dropping his cigarette butt over the edge then pulling his phone out of his back pocket.

So the lad hadn't twigged he'd pushed them? Good.

"I have no idea. We should call for help." He snatched the phone off him, switched it off, and stuffed it into his bomber jacket pocket.

"Oi. Stop messing about. We need to ring the bloody police or something." Stephan stepped forward, hand out, ready to receive his property.

He walked away from the kid, farther inland. "Mobiles don't work up here, this close to the sea. I'll ring from my house. It's just along the way a bit." He stared at the woods where the hollow resided deep inside, hoping the lad followed him. After a few metres, the sound of footsteps on the grass drew closer. He turned, Stephan right behind him.

He punched him in the mouth.

Down the teen went.

"Don't make this difficult," he said, staring at Stephan. "You need God and Jesus. They will help you."

Stephan gawped back. "You're fucking mental, you are."

108

Another punch.

That one shut him up. Now all that was left was to get him home.

To the cellar.

He'd been down in the cellar a few times to collect stuff for Grandmother. So many things were stored there. A box of vinyl records which she played on her old-fashioned stereo. A crate full of the best china for when her cronies came round for a posh dinner. A bottle of wine from the ancient wooden rack, cobwebs draped over the necks. But he hadn't expected to stay down there.

After she'd let him out of the tree, she'd given him 'the speech', and he'd agreed to go along with her, just to shut her up. Once he was home, he'd been tempted to tell Mum where he'd really been – not staying a couple of nights over at Grandmother's like he'd been told to say, but inside a tree, for Pete's sake, hanging there like Jesus on the cross. She wouldn't have believed that anyway, saying he was making up stories.

After Grandmother's sermon, she'd said, "What you endured, I endured, and it hasn't done me any harm. We're godly people, boy, and when we pass over, Jesus will be waiting by the gates, not St Peter. No, we deserve Jesus to greet us."

He hadn't quite been the disciple she'd wanted at first. He'd tried, honestly he had, but she'd said another stint of penance was needed, and she'd rung Mum and told her he was staying over again. For three nights – Friday, Saturday, Sunday, and he'd go to school from her house on Monday.

And he'd been brought down here, chained to the wall, although unlike in the tree, the chains had enough links to allow him to walk around but not reach any of the dusty boxes or their contents. A large picture of the scary Jesus was taped to the wall opposite him, fresh and new amongst the antique belongings.

He stared at the wine, wishing he could pick up a bottle and unscrew the lid, drinking it just so his mouth wasn't dry. Red wine, all of it, the blood of Christ. But his metre circumference wouldn't allow it, so he slumped onto the old mattress that didn't have a sheet on it and pulled the coarse grey blanket over himself. The green robe wasn't enough to keep out the chill, and at one point he was so distraught he contemplated using the rope belt to hang himself from the rafter directly above, but there was nothing close by for him to stand on to get up there. And it would hurt Mum, so he gathered his strength and endured the confinement, starving, thirsty, crapping and pissing in a shallow tray Grandmother had left for him.

After what he guessed was two days – it must have been Sunday, and wasn't that poignant? – Grandmother appeared at the top of the open-slat stairs, the light from the doorway spilling down, showing up dust motes for the hovering bastards they

110

were. She descended and came to stand just outside his free space.

"Have you learnt anything?" she asked.

He'd learnt he needed food and drink, a bath, and a new grandmother, but he kept that to himself. That was the Devil talking. "I must follow God and Jesus, no matter what."

"Good boy. What else?"

"That I must be humble and allow the teachings into my life." It was what she'd said in the speech, so he scrabbled to remember more. "I must embrace religion and go to confession weekly, as well as mass."

"Excellent. Do you pledge to obey the Lord throughout your life?"

He nodded, wondering if his father had been subjected to this. Had he killed himself because of Grandmother and what she'd put him through? Had his mind broken and he couldn't stand the horror of the memories? He understood how that could happen. He was broken himself now, although there was still a tiny nugget of him resenting her, hating her, railing against what she expected of him.

"Every time you stray from the path, I'll put you in the hollow or down here," she said. "Do you understand?"

He did. "Yes."

"Then let's get you in the bath and cleaned up. You may eat only when you've washed. Jesus doesn't like filth."

The Devil prodded for him to say Jesus was meant to love everyone no matter what they smelt like, but he didn't have the energy to fight her.

He bathed, he ate, and listened to her rambling on the chaise in the drawing room, reading passages from her beloved crow, her fingers gripping the wings, the words meshing, making no sense. His head bobbed from tiredness, yet still she blathered, until her mantel clock chimed midnight.

"Off to bed," she said. "Sleep on how you've shunned God and Jesus. Wake up tomorrow, baptised and new. If you don't, your mother will suffer. I won't help her with money. Life will become difficult."

So he'd done it for her, his beautiful mum, and life had never been the same again.

Stephan was a wisp of a thing really. Slim, low weight, so carrying him home hadn't been an issue. He'd put him in the cellar, on the same mattress, which was disgusting now, but needs must. The boy was still out of it, so he put the robe on over his clothes and placed Grandad's slippers on his feet, still damp and stinking of piss from when Jayden had them on. He'd collected them from the hollow on his way back through the woods before he'd come out again to stand on the cliff in Dad's spot.

He really had been contemplating God, among other things, and the kids coming by had seemed like an answer to his prayers. God also wanted him to bring a new person into the fold, that much was clear.

The fact he'd pushed the girls off…that stuck in his craw a bit. Still, it couldn't be helped, not if he'd wanted to take Stephan. And it was done now.

"No use crying over spilt milk," Grandmother said, hands on hips beside him.

"What do *you* want?" he groused, ensuring the cuffs were secure around Stephan's wrists.

"I'm here to see you do this properly. You messed it up with Jayden. The police will be all over that in a second. You'd better hope you didn't leave anything of yourself behind."

His heart leapt, and he thought back to when he'd taken Jayden to the park. "No, I even cleaned the phone."

"Right. There are fibres these days. Microscopic. But they can be found."

"Why are you telling me that? You're meant to want this as much as I do. Scaring me isn't doing me any favours."

"Why should you have favours? I know what's in that black heart of yours. You claim to love God and our dear Jesus, yet you think terrible things."

He did, and they were mainly about her. How she'd taken his life away. How she'd moulded him over the years into a man who put children inside trees and cellars. This wasn't right. Was it?

She says it is.

"I do," she said. "It's exactly right. This boy here needs our Lord." She gripped his chin and forced him to look at her. "And *you're* going to bring Him into his life. Where's the toilet tray?"

He glanced around. There it was, hanging on a hook below the picture of the scary Jesus on his pedestal, one he'd pinned up there just yesterday. He collected it and placed it inside the free-walking zone.

"Now you need to write the note," she urged. "Do it quickly. He's stirring. You don't have your face covered—and what a stupid mistake that was; you did it at the cliff, too. Stephan can identify you now. You can't send him home. He has to stay here forever."

"Shut. Up." He didn't need a reminder of how he'd messed up. Angry with himself, and with her for pointing it out, he raced upstairs and scribbled down the words—he knew them off by heart. After all, he'd read them enough times while in the cellar himself. It even looked like Grandmother's writing, as though she'd channelled herself into him.

He shivered at the thought.

Back in the cellar, he placed the note in the zone then left, Grandmother trailing him up the stairs. He locked the door then moved into the kitchen to drink the blood of Christ, a whole bottle of it, pausing every so often to eat the sacramental bread he'd made himself.

Jesus was with him now, in body and spirit, so he weaved into the drawing room and knelt before the scary version, praying Stephan would be the one to follow in his footsteps.

"You are a bad man," his teen self whispered.

Jesus stared at him with his maniacal eyes.

"Leave me alone," he said. "Please, just leave me alone."

CHAPTER TWELVE

Helena once again sat at the island in Katherine's kitchen. Dave Lund had come after Helena had texted him, and Andy stood by the door. Dave perched beside Katherine, who cried, leaning into him. He held her close, and Helena couldn't stand hearing the sobs wrenching out of her. She got up and busied herself sorting tea, giving that poor mother some time to let the first wave of grief out. She looked like she hadn't slept since the night before Jayden had gone missing, the bags under her eyes puffy and daubed with shadows.

Drinks made, Helena took them to the island and placed the cups down. While Katherine continued mourning, Helena, Andy, and Dave drank their tea. To anyone watching it would appear heartless, but from experience, they all knew to just let the bereft cry it out. No good would come of trying to talk to her right now.

A good fifteen minutes passed, then Katherine composed herself, her face blotchy, her eyes even redder than they'd been previously. She pulled herself upright, away from Dave, but he kept his arm around her shoulders. Katherine picked up her mug and drank, the brew undoubtedly tepid now, but Helena didn't offer to make a fresh one. Best to let the woman do things her own way.

"Why my boy?" Katherine asked. Then, "Oh God, I need to tell Will…"

"Give Andy the details," Helena said gently. "He can make sure Will is contacted. Would you prefer Will to ring you so you can tell him, or would you like his superior officer to do it?"

"The officer," she said. "If I hear his voice, I'll crack."

"Okay."

Katherine told them which regiment her husband was in, and Andy walked out to make the call. Nothing else was said until he returned.

"They're going to get in contact with him," Andy said. "He'll obviously be allowed home."

Whether that was now or whenever the gears of the army worked, Helena didn't like to ask.

Not in front of Katherine. She had enough to contend with.

"Will you allow someone to come and stay with you now?" Helena asked.

Katherine nodded. "My mum and dad." She looked at Andy. "Will you ring Mum? I can't… I just…"

"Of course. Would you like me to tell her, or just ask her to come and stay?"

"They live around the corner. Just say I need her. Her name's Geraldine."

Helena thought it so strange that Katherine hadn't had her mother here long before now, and she asked why.

"Because I thought…I thought if I kept it quiet, it wouldn't be true."

You're very lucky it hasn't made the news yet and your mum found out that way. But Helena understood the woman's reasoning. She'd done similar after she'd escaped from Uthway. If she didn't talk about it, it meant it didn't happen, except her mind had other ideas, and it had forced her not only to remember but into therapy. Bullied her into facing it all and getting it into perspective so she could cope in everyday life.

Andy walked out again, and his indecipherable words filtered through, a low hum that seemed comforting somehow. He was *doing* something, helping, while Helena felt like a spare part, useless and without the words to comfort Jayden's mother. What could she say? 'I'm sorry for your loss' didn't seem adequate, not when it was a child who had died.

"Was…was he hurt?" Katherine asked.

Helena glanced at Dave to get some feedback on whether he thought she could handle the truth. He nodded.

"He had split lips and a bleeding nose, so we think he was struck." She waited a beat to see how that had gone down. *She's okay so far.* "And he'd been held with some kind of bonds on his wrists."

"Oh Christ…"

"Do you want me to continue?"

"Yes."

"He has a contusion on the back of his head, but it's not clear what caused it—the post-mortem will help us determine that. It seems he struggled for breath near the end."

"Asthma. He has asthma."

Why didn't you tell us that until now? "And there were no signs of sexual assault, although he was found in only his boxers and socks."

"What? If no one touched him like…like that, why were his clothes removed?"

"We don't know. We came straight here after we went to see him. Traces of where he'd been could have transferred to the fabric, so they were perhaps removed. Officers will be

120

searching the woods and the surrounding areas for his clothing and shoes. Would he have had a school bag?"

"Yes, a blue backpack."

"What sort of blue?"

"Navy. It's Nike."

"Okay." A whoosh of cold air came in, and Helena assumed Andy was going outside to wait for the mother and father. "Now some time has passed, have you thought more on who could have abducted him?"

"There's no one. Speak to Dad. He's a solicitor. Could it be to do with that?"

Helena nodded. "Maybe." *Disgruntled clients or their family members?*

The clatter of footsteps in the hall had Helena stiffening her spine and drawing enough courage to face another upset female. Andy came in, a woman and man following.

"Mum!" Katherine said, her voice strangled.

"Whatever's happened, love? Is it Will?" Geraldine asked, clutching Katherine and drawing her close so Dave's arm fell away.

"It's Jayden. Oh God…" Katherine stared at Helena. "You tell them. I thought I could but…I can't…"

"Jayden?" the man asked.

"Your name, sir?" Helena smiled wanly, recognising him from being in the station a few times but for the life of her she couldn't recall his name.

"Neil Yates," he said, holding a hand out. "Helena Stratton, yes?"

"Yes," she said. "I'm sorry to see you again under such circumstances."

"And those circumstances are?" Neil cocked his head.

"I hate to have to say this, but Jayden went missing after school yesterday. His body was found this evening in the park."

"What?" Geraldine shrieked.

"His *body*?" Neil said.

"I'm afraid so." Helena hung her head for a moment.

"Please come and speak to me in the living room," Neil said.

Helena agreed—she could inform him of everything, and he could pass on what he felt the women could handle. Helena closed the living room door. They sat, and Helena recounted everything. It was safe, Neil being a solicitor—he was unlikely to bandy the information about, knowing how that could affect the case.

"Dear Lord," Neil said, rubbing his chin, his eyes misty.

Helena imagined Jayden would have looked like him had he been given the chance to grow up.

"And the note?" he mused. "Why was Jayden let go a day early? It doesn't make sense that someone would be specific about a day, then go back on it."

"Katherine mentioned Jayden had asthma. I'm wondering, and it could be a long shot, whether he didn't have access to his inhaler and had a severe attack he didn't recover from. Those are the first indications regarding cause of death. Of course, I didn't know he had asthma at the time I spoke to the ME, but it makes sense now."

"Maybe the abductor panicked. It wouldn't be the first time someone has died by accident," Neil said.

"No, but whoever took him is still the cause. If Jayden had been at home, he'd have had his Ventolin handy. He wasn't, so the abductor, in my eyes, is as culpable as if he'd shot him— sorry to sound so cruel."

"I agree, and I understand what you're saying. I prefer practicality, the blunt approach. Soft-soaping doesn't wash with me."

She guessed he hadn't realised he'd made a pun.

"Good, then we're on the same page." *Or we're in the same bathwater. No, that's not appropriate, Helena…*

"It's damn annoying the CCTV outside the station didn't pick up the person's face," Neil said.

"Isn't it just. I'm waiting on forensics regarding the note, so hopefully they'll get a shift on and we can—" Her phone rang. "Excuse me a moment." She swiped her screen. "What's up, Clive?"

"Bodies."

"You what?" What the fuck was going on here?

"Two teen girls seem to have cliff-jumped, landed on a ledge. The helicopter went out and winched them up. Both dead."

"Bloody hell."

"And there's more. A lad called Stephan Korby didn't come home this evening."

"Oh no… Uniform are round there speaking to the family?"

"Yes."

"Tell them to stay there this time, no palming it off like they did before." She'd almost said 'with Jayden' but remembered Neil was listening to every word. "I'll be there as soon as I can. I'll go to the other location afterwards, okay? Zach there?"

"Yes, guv."

"Address?"

He recited it.

"Okay, tarra for now." She put her phone in her pocket.

Neil stared at her, his cheeks blanching. "Another child has gone missing, hasn't it?"

She nodded. "A lad. Christ Almighty."

"If it's the same person who's taken him, you might get another note," he said.

Helena massaged her temples. "I'll have to use my phone again for a second, sorry." She rang Clive. "It's Helena. Watch that front door, got it? We could be getting another note. This time I want them caught when they post it. When you go off shift, pass that on to whoever takes over from you, okay?"

"Yep, will do."

She cut the call. "I'm going to have to go. Andy and Dave will need to come with me. Can you manage without a FLO?"

Neil bobbed his head. "Yes. I'll take care of them, don't worry. Just...just get out there and do what needs to be done."

She patted his arm then returned to the kitchen. "Andy, Dave..."

They stared at her, picking up on what had happened. Damn, they were good at reading her. "Katherine, Geraldine, we need to go. Dave can come back at some point tomorrow if you need him." *Providing he can leave Stephan's parents.*

Katherine shook her head. "No, it's okay. Dad's here now."

Her phone rang.

Everyone stared at it.

Katherine looked at the screen. "Oh no. It's Will."

Neil came in. "I'll get it." And to Helena, kindly, "Go."

They left, Andy getting in her car, Dave following them to Stephan's address. Life in the lad's house would be upside down and inside out, and they would be walking into an emotional war zone. She was nervous on the journey but told herself this one could just be a case of a boy staying out past his curfew.

She could only hope that was the case.

Her gut screamed it wasn't, and she clenched the steering wheel tighter.

Upon arrival, she took a moment to calm herself, then knocked on the door. A uniform answered and quietly whispered the parents' names—Julie and Martin—then showed them to a living room.

A woman, brunette, slender, a scrunched-up tissue in hand, sat on a chair opposite the door. A man was on the sofa, a child either side of him, his arms around their shoulders. A second uniform stood by the window.

"Have you found him?" Julie asked.

"I'm afraid not." Helena smiled sadly. "I need to ask some questions, much like the officers here have already asked, I suspect, but I need to know as much about Stephan as you can give me."

"He's been taken like that Jayden kid, hasn't he?" Martin asked.

Shit. Of course word would have spread. Ben or his mum, Shona Long and her mother, other kids at the school finding out the police had been asking questions in Queensley's office, Queensley himself...people talked.

"I'm going to be treating it as such, yes," Helena said, "but that doesn't mean that's the case. I don't want to assume he's just missed his usual time of coming home. It's best to work on the safe side. Do you have a picture we can take of Stephan?"

One of the officers handed a scanned one over.

Helena almost groaned. She'd seen this kid at the park. He'd been the one she'd cautioned about a pickled liver. "Just give me a moment, okay?"

She left the room and went into the kitchen, closing the door. Then she rang Clive. "Listen, I'm at Stephan's house. I recognised him as one of the lads at the park when we went down to see Jayden in situ. There were five kids altogether—one of them was a Shona Long, a

127

girl who'd walked home with Ben Griffin on the afternoon Jayden was taken. I'm worried she might be one of the girls on the cliff. Her mum's name is Christine. Do a search for me and call her. Ask her if Shona is home, but make out it's in relation to the questions I asked them at the park to do with Jayden."

"Will do."

She returned to the living room, acting as though nothing was amiss, and questioned Julie and Martin about their son. Stephan had apparently gone off the rails a bit lately, drinking and smoking, acting up, but not to the degree his parents were overly worried. They felt it was just the lad segueing into the teenage years and he'd settle down once he realised booze and fags weren't all that clever. Other than a few grunts as responses and a small amount of rudeness, he was a good kid.

"Andy will go up and look in his room now," Helena said.

Andy walked out.

"I've already done it, guv," an officer said.

"Best to double-check." If these were the same two who'd visited Katherine, acting half-arsed about things, she didn't want to leave anything solely to them. "Now, Dave here is a family liaison officer. If you want him to stay with you for a couple of hours to explain things…?"

Martin nodded. "Please. It's all so bloody worrying. We don't know what to do."

"Dave will tell you what happens in these situations so you know what to expect," Helena said. "Ask any questions, however insignificant you think they are. Never think you're being a pest, okay? This is your child — nothing is more important than him at the moment, all right?"

Martin nodded, Julie burst into tears, and Andy reappeared. He shook his head — so Stephan's room was no cause for alarm. Good.

"We need to go now. Oh, one more thing." Helena stopped by the doorway. "Do you know who he was out with this evening?"

"Probably Shona," Julie said, sniffling. "She's his girlfriend."

Fucking hell… "Okay. Anyone else?"

Julie shook her head.

"Right. Well, I'll be in touch." Helena gestured for the two officers to leave with her and Andy, and, out by her car, she told them, "Go and start door-to-door along here, see if anyone saw Stephan and who he was with when he left here at five. After that, go to help the others on the cliff top. People on the estate that backs on to it will need speaking to as well. Tell Clive where you are — he's on the front desk at the moment."

They nodded.

129

Helena and Andy got into the car. She messaged Zach to see if he was at the cliff top. He wrote back—yes, he was; Jayden had been taken to the morgue. He sent a picture of the dead girls.

"Oh no…" she said.

"What's up?" Andy asked.

"One of the girls on the cliff is Shona Long." She rang Clive. "Did you get hold of Catherine Long?"

"No answer. I'm assuming she's out or something."

"Fuck it. Okay, don't call her again. We're going to the cliffs. Her daughter is one of them."

"Christ."

"I know. I'll ring you soon." Then she called Ol, Phil, and Evan. They were needed—this couldn't wait until the morning. She related all that had happened and set them their tasks to begin as soon as they arrived in the incident room.

It was going to be one hell of a long night.

CHAPTER THIRTEEN

Stephan woke to find himself in a weird room, a little brass lantern casting meagre light on the floor beside him. Boxes in stacks opposite. Blue plastic crates full of junk—a teapot spout protruded from one of them, a dirty, pink feather duster from another. A wine rack—the only thing that wasn't covered in cobwebs. Above it on the wall was a plaque: *The Blood of Christ, our Saviour.*

What the heck was that all about?

His heart sped up. What was he doing here?

His wrists hurt, so he peered down at them. Cuffs, metal, with long chains attached to the wall beside him. And he was lying on a scabby old mattress that stank of…he wasn't sure what it was. Mould?

And what was this he had on over his clothes? A green dress? As for the checked slippers, they weren't his.

He sat up, confused, dazed, and remembered swigging cheapo cider with Shona and the others. He must have got drunk and blacked out, and this was a dream. Then a recollection popped up—they'd gone to the cliff after being at the park, and this weirdo had been there, banging on about God. Then Shona and Clara had bloody jumped over, and that man had snatched Stephan's phone, walking off with it.

Stephan shuddered.

He'd been punched. The memory brought on a sharp pain in his lip, and he licked it, the bump of a scab evident.

Had the mad bloke brought him here?

"Help!" he called out, glancing over at some stairs made out of wooden slats, more boxes piled beneath. A basement?

Beside the boxes…a Smaltern Secondary school uniform, shoes, and a Nike backpack, and he all but crapped himself.

"Help!"

Frantic, he got up and made to walk across the room, but the chains weren't long enough, keeping him inside an invisible perimeter. He caught sight of a picture above one of the box stacks. Jesus. Staring. Like he was as mental as the man on the cliff. Stephan turned his attention to the wrist cuffs, inspecting them to see if he could get them undone or pull his hands through them, but they needed keys. His palms had red on them, like blood, and he gawped at it, his bladder threatening to release all that cider.

What the fuck?

He flopped down onto the mattress, and a folded piece of paper kicked up from the displaced air. He grabbed it, opened it, and read the spidery writing in the feeble light.

Jesus belongs in your life. He is who you should aspire to be – good, holy, selfless. You will learn humility, and you will thank me for what I have done. You are required in the fold, and you shall sit on a pew every Sunday and read the Bible each night before bed. There is no compromise. You will love Jesus and our Lord, God, without question.

Stephan frowned. It *was* the cliff man; he *had* taken him. He didn't know anyone else who talked about Jesus and whatever in this way.

Suddenly and without warning, tears came. He wasn't so tough now, the bolshy lad he'd become disappearing, revealing the still-vulnerable and needy child within, the boy who'd gone to Mum when he'd hurt himself, who'd gone to Dad when he needed a cuddle if he'd been bullied in his younger years.

The tears fell for ages, only stopping at the sound of a door opening, and Stephan's heart leapt. Had the police found him? A shaft of brightness fell over the stairs, showing up the filthy wall and the dirty handrail. Two feet appeared, then legs as the person came down, the slats creaking, the noise of them grating on Stephan's nerves.

Whoever this was… Shit, a balaclava covered his head and face. Eyes sat inside cut-out circles, wide and glaring. A mouth…thick lips protruded from another hole. Was this the God-loving twat who'd stolen his phone?

"Who are you?" Stephan asked, sounding about five years old and hating it, wishing he could be stronger, like his dad.

"I'm here to light your way."

"Light my way?"

The man held a book in both hands, and he bowed his head. "You need guidance. I'm here to teach you. I shall read from the crow."

The crow?

The bloke sat outside the perimeter, cross-legged, and opened the black book. He recited passages Stephan recognised, from at school maybe, religious. Was 'the crow' a Bible? Mark, Luke, Mary, Jesus, all the names blurred in his head as they sat there for what he imagined were hours, the man droning on, Stephan losing focus at times, almost drifting off.

"Do *not* sleep. You must remain awake and listen. You can only sleep when I say so, when Jesus tells me to stop reading."

Jesus ought to hurry the hell up and say something then, because Stephan's eyes had a mind of their own. They kept shutting, and he had no control over them.

"Wake up!" the bloke shouted.

Stephan jolted, eyes springing open, and he slapped his forehead in an attempt to become alert. The chains tinkled, reminding him he was locked up, held captive.

"I want to go home," he wailed.

"Not yet. Not until you've agreed to follow the Lord."

"I will. I'll follow him. I'll do whatever you say. I just want my mum…"

"Soon. Now shut up. *If I speak in the tongues of men or of angels, but do not have love, I am only a resounding gong or a clanging cymbal.*"

What the fuck did gongs and cymbals have to do with anything?

The bloke carried on, spouting stuff about the gift of prophecy, fathoming mysteries, and moving mountains. Stephan zoned out—it was too much to take in. He thought about his little brother and sister at home, tucked up in bed. Mum and Dad would be well worried by now, maybe even angry he hadn't come home. And what about Shona and Clara? They'd be dead, surely, what with jumping off that cliff.

Fresh tears fell, and his chest tightened.

What seemed like eons later, the man stood. "That is all the crow will tell you for today. Sleep. Think about Jesus and how you will embrace him. In the morning, you shall learn more lessons."

Stephan was too exhausted to say anything. He curled up on the mattress and drew an itchy grey blanket over him. The man switched off the little brass lantern, then plodded up the stairs, closing the door, which shut off the spilling light.

Stephan welcomed the darkness.

He locked the cellar door and hung the key on a brass cup hook screwed into the jamb. Weary, his throat dry from speaking for so long, he went into the kitchen and opened a bottle of blood of Christ. At the table, he drank goblet after goblet, the alcohol streaming through his own blood, the two mixing so Jesus was inside him, a part of him. He'd make bread tomorrow—not enough for five thousand, but enough for him and Stephan.

"You shouldn't feed him," Grandmother said, plonking herself in the opposite chair and grabbing the bottle. She drank straight from it, which was most unlike her. She'd learnt some bad habits in Hell, it seemed. "If you give him food, he won't be so eager to obey you."

He had to feed him, though, to make up for what had happened to Jayden. That had been such a terrible mistake, and if Jesus found out what he'd done, he'd be damned to join Grandmother in Hell. There would be no Heaven for him.

"I have to make amends. Atone for my sins," he said.

"You'll amend by bringing Stephan into Jesus' arms." She swigged from the bottle again.

"That won't fix what I did to those girls, though."

"That was an error of judgement," she said. "But I suspect they would have grown up to be women of the street or some such vile thing. Jezebels. Working for the Devil. You did them a favour. They're in Heaven now."

He wanted to believe her, but the very Devil she'd mentioned was perched on his shoulder now, wittering on about how murdering three children wasn't what God would want, but the Devil...he enjoyed that sort of thing.

Confused, he sipped at Jesus' blood. It was becoming commonplace now, to drink more and more of it instead of just on Sundays. He baked the sacramental wafers often, ate too many of them, all because he was worried if he didn't fill himself up with their goodness, he'd wander off the righteous path.

"You're such a stupid man," Grandmother said. "You're letting him in, aren't you? What have I told you about The Evil One? He will find the cracks and slither through them, staining your godly soul. Corrupting."

"That's what you do," he said. "You corrupted me as a teenager, just like I'm trying to corrupt Stephan." His teen self was rearing his head. Getting bold.

"I *saved* you," she said.

He got up from the table and left her drinking liquid Jesus, stumbling up the stairs, half mad with his tormenting thoughts. He flung himself beneath the duvet and hid, but the voices carried on—the Devil and Grandmother.

"I'm going to let Stephan go tomorrow," he whispered.

"No," Grandmother shouted.

"Kill him," the Devil said.

Was this what it felt like to go crazy? To have people who didn't exist talking to you? To have three sides of yourself? Good, evil, and his old teen self?

He shut his eyes and thought of Mum. Should he sell up and move to be closer to her? Start a new life, putting all this mess behind him? If it wasn't for Grandmother appearing, telling him to take a boy and put him in the tree, he would have continued his boring life, the one she'd created — work, church, choir practise, prayers, rinse and repeat.

Sleep took a while to come, but as he drifted off, he remembered he hadn't done something. He shot out of bed and ran downstairs, collecting today's newspaper from the drawing room.

At the kitchen table, he composed a note for the police.

Julie Korby watched the clock. Eleven at night. Dave Lund had been a great help. To be honest, Julie didn't know what they'd have done without his calming influence. Martin would have got agitated, and they might have rowed, their nerves too frayed to stop spiteful things coming out of their mouths:

You should have told him to get back inside once you said he wasn't allowed out.

If you'd backed me up, he wouldn't have thought he could ignore me, would he?

It's your fault he's not here.

No, it's yours.

It would have escalated. They'd have said things they didn't mean. With Dave talking to them, explaining what the police would be doing right now to bring Stephan home, it meant they had hope. Something to focus on. Jayden Rook being found dead, though... Was that Stephan's fate, too?

Julie shivered and imagined her boy in a nice bed somewhere, fast asleep, content, unharmed. She smiled. It would be okay — it had to be. If Stephan didn't come home... She couldn't believe that. Dave said to remain positive, despite the odds, so that was what she'd do.

You're going to be fine, son, just you wait and see.

CHAPTER FOURTEEN

It had taken ages to be able to have a look at the girls on the cliff. With so many in authority involved — the helicopter, officers, paramedics, Zach, even the coastguard had turned up — it had been manic. Now, with the ambulance gone because it wasn't needed, and all extra people leaving the scene, the tent and lights had been erected. Zach was inside, taking their temperatures. SOCO were about, spectre-like in their white suits. One had been winched down to the ledge to take pictures of the blood on the rock.

If only those children had gone home when she'd told them to leave the park instead of coming up here. She had Stephan and Shona

141

down as positive identifications, but the second girl, no clue, and who were the other two lads who'd been with them earlier?

She should have taken their names when she'd spoken to them. An officer on duty at the park had reported to Clive that he hadn't written their names down either, just asked them to move along, which they hadn't.

Mistakes were a pest.

It was quarter past eleven, and she didn't want to go inside the tent yet so called the incident room. Ol answered.

"Hi, it's me. Found anything we can use?"

"Not much on Facebook—they're on it but don't seem to use it very often. Instagram is another matter. We have Stephan's password, given to us by Dave, and I was able to see Shona's images as well as a few others. Shona appears to be best friends with a girl called Clara, but there's no mention of a second name."

"She spoke to Ben and Shona on the day they walked home from school together. I might give Ben's mum a ring to see if she knows this Clara's surname, although I doubt it. She made it quite clear she didn't even know Shona when Ben mentioned it at the school. I'd have to get her to ask Ben. Can you send me her number, please."

"Yep, will do it now. In other news, Stephan's phone is off."

"Figures."

"Clive has gone home — Louise is back on the front desk. She's watching out for another note to arrive."

"Whoever it is would be a bit of a dick to post a second one by hand."

"Some people are so full of themselves they fail to think of the obvious, though. Maybe this person feels they're invincible."

"Hmm. So is that it for now?"

"Yes. CCTV has thrown nothing up for Evan and Phil. They've checked as close to the park as they can, but the cliff top has nothing either, obviously, and the only cameras on the estate backing onto it are at the two strips of local shops. The kids aren't on it, so they must have got their alcohol elsewhere — you know, they didn't hang about outside the shops to talk an adult into buying it, which is all the rage these days."

"So get them to look at all the local shops on every estate, just in case they did that elsewhere. Have they checked the actual town yet?"

"Yes. No kids at all, just adults going into pubs and restaurants."

"Okay, well, keep at it. I'm just about to ring Mrs Griffin then go and see the girls." Helena paused. "In the tent."

"I don't envy you."

"Be glad you're at the station. Bye now."
Helena checked WhatsApp for Ol's message,
then dialled the number.

It took a while, but Goldie Hawn answered,
her voice thick, sleep-riddled. "Who is this?"

"Sorry to disturb you so late, but it's DI
Helena Stratton—I met you at the school."

"Oh. You."

Rude.

"Yes. Me. I need you to ask Ben something for
me."

"But he's asleep!"

"I realise that, but it's important to the
investigation."

Goldie sighed. "What is it?"

"I need to know the surname of Clara, the one
Ben and Shona stopped to talk to."

"*Tsk.* Hold on." Shuffling. Footsteps. A door
creaking open. Another door. "Ben!"

"What?"

"Don't you dare speak to me in that stroppy
voice. The police are on the phone. What's that
Clara girl's name?"

"Bates. Go away."

A door slammed.

"Did you get that?" Goldie asked.

"I did. Thank you. Again, I apologise for
having to disturb you."

"Have you found Jayden yet?"

Helena debated whether to tell her or not. *Sod it.* "Yes. Unfortunately, he's deceased."

"I beg your pardon?"

"I'm afraid so. I must get on. I advise you not to let Ben out after school for the time being. Another lad went missing tonight."

"Good grief! What is the world coming to?"

"I have to go. Goodbye." She ended that call and made another to Ol. "Hi, her name's Clara Bates. Can you send me a picture of her off Instagram, just in case it's the other dead girl here?"

"Will do."

"Also send me her home address. I really must get in that tent. Catch you soon."

She slid her phone away and walked towards the flaps. Andy milled about chatting to various SOCOs, and she called him quietly, the halogen lamps on tall metal poles illuminating the scene in a ghastly manner—bright white on SOCO suits; highlighted puffs of cloud-breaths coming from mouths; the grass an eerie green, too pronounced, the colour of a garish crayon.

They entered the tent together, and four SOCOs hunkered down checking the grass, Tom one of them. He waved, and she returned the gesture, then headed for Zach and the girls. Her phone bleeped, so she checked it. Ol had sent the image and address. She stared at the girl smiling from her phone screen and sighed.

Helena moved to stand beside Shona, whose long hair was splayed around her head, her eyes closed, her face sporting a livid purple bruise on one side where she'd hit the ledge.

The other girl...was Clara.

"Hi," Zach said and looked up at her. He was annoyed—a frown, mouth pursed.

"What's the matter?"

"I'm a bit narked at a decision that was made by the police in the helicopter, although I can kind of understand it."

"What did they do?"

"Winched the girls up straight away—no leaving them on the ledge once they realised they were dead. No photos of them in situ. I would have been able to tell things from their landing positions, which way they faced when they went over, that kind of thing. One of the officers gave me a brief description, but the decision was made to lift them up as the ledge isn't big enough for more than one person and the two girls to have fitted on."

"Hmm. Do you think they decided to just jump?" she asked.

"No. Slight bruising coming up on their backs—faint, but there. Fingertip marks. I'd say they were pushed. Bloody hard."

"Christ. How long ago?"

"An estimate, based on the cold...between now and three hours ago."

"So it could have been about eight-fifteen," she said. "Stephan is usually due home at nine. So close to making it there."

Andy coughed and turned away.

"You all right?" she asked him.

"Yeah. It was what you said. Forty-five minutes, and he'd have been safe."

"There are so many aspects here. I'm beating myself up about the fact I sent them away from the park and they didn't go straight home. There were two other lads with them. We need to find out who they are."

"What, you think kids did this? Took Jayden and Stephan?"

"We have to consider it, surely. Look at all those gangs they have in London and other big cities. It could be spreading to places like this, kids joining them, doing things they don't want to do but doing it anyway, otherwise the gang leaders will hurt them."

"We'd know if we had gangs here," Andy said.

"Would we, though? We don't know who's selling the drugs yet or who the pimp is sending women out at night. We don't know where Uthway has sloped off to."

"I see your point."

"I know it's mad to think it's kids, but we can't discount it. The station CCTV of the person who left the note…that could be a year ten or eleven, easily. Have you seen the *size* of some of these kids today?"

Andy nodded. Sighed. "Where are we going first?"

"To Shona Long's."

"Any news from the team?"

"Basically, no."

He shook his head. Turned back to face the girls. "Fucking shocking waste of life."

"I know." Helena patted his back.

She drove to the Long's place and parked out the front. It was an average-looking house, no airs and graces but neat enough — clean windows, a tidy front garden, a green wheelie bin that appeared as though it got cleaned every week or two. She knocked on the door, cringing at the late hour and what was to come. It took several more knocks for a light to go on, possibly the landing, then another in the hallway, shining through the glass in the front door.

A woman stood there in pink fleece pyjamas, her long, dark hair bedraggled on one side, giving a tumbleweed effect. "Yes?"

"Hello. I'm DI Helena Stratton, I spoke to you on the phone, and this is DS Andy Mald. We're here about Shona."

"Oh, bloody hell. What's she done?" She rubbed one eye, smearing the black liner she hadn't washed off before bed.

"It's better that we come in."

"All right…" Long stepped back and led them into a kitchen at the end of the hallway. She flicked on the light and moved to the kettle.

"Andy will do that," Helena said. "Let's sit down, shall we?"

Long frowned but chose a seat at the table in the dining area. "What's going on?"

"You don't seem surprised Shona isn't home tonight," Helena started.

"Why should I? She's staying over at Clara's. Clara Bates. What have they got themselves into?"

Heaven. "I saw them at the park earlier with three other people, lads. They were drinking cider and smoking."

"Oh, bloody hell." Long slapped the table. "She didn't get it from us, I can assure you — the fags and booze."

"Us?"

"Me and her dad. He's in bed, out for the count. He wouldn't hear a herd of elephants tromp through once he's asleep."

"Where were you this evening?"

"We went out for a meal." Long blushed. "Might sound stupid when we're this age, but we have date nights."

"Not stupid at all. Did you have your phone on?"

"Yes, but if it isn't Shona calling on date night, I don't answer."

149

"I see. We tried to call you…"

"So *that's* who it was."

The kettle came to a noisy, rattling boil. The sound of Andy pouring the water was so normal, at odds with what Helena had come here to say.

"So what happens now?" Long blinked, as though she struggled to comprehend her daughter knocking back cider and drawing nicotine into her body. "Don't you usually just take the drink and cigarettes away and send them off with a warning?"

So this has happened before?

"That's not why we're here." *I wish it was.* "Does Shona have a curfew?"

"Yes, ten o'clock."

"So it would be plausible for her to be on the cliff top around that time, yes?"

"Yes, but she's not meant to go up there. It's too dangerous. And I'm sure Clara has to be in by nine, so Shona would have to follow those rules, seeing as she's staying at their house."

"Stephan Korby…"

"Yes, he's a lad she's seeing. Nice boy. He comes round for dinner sometimes, but she hasn't had the courage to go to his yet."

"They got along?"

"Yes." Long narrowed her eyes. "*Got?*"

Helena ignored that slip of the tongue. "So they didn't argue?"

"Not that I know of. Why?"

Because I'm trying to work out if it's likely he pushed your daughter and her friend off the bloody cliff, pissed out of his head, then did a runner.

Andy brought the tea over, placing it in front of Long.

"Thanks," she said, picking it up and blowing on it. "Didn't you two want one?"

"No, thank you." Helena had been about to tell her what she was really here for, but she waited until Long had taken a sip and put the cup back down.

"I'm sorry, but we have some terrible news," she said.

"Like what?" Long's eyebrows shot up.

"Two bodies were found on a cliff ledge this evening. From my visual identification, one of them is Shona."

Long remained silent, staring at something behind Helena. Andy? "Can you say that again, please?"

Helena didn't need to. The woman crumpled, and a wail came soaring out of her, heavy with grief and fear. Her face screwed up, and tears sprouted. Helena turned to look at Andy, pointing to the ceiling. He left the kitchen, and the *clomp* of his footsteps on the stairs sounded far too loud.

While Long cried, Helena held her hand until Andy reappeared with a man beside him, who rushed to his wife, tears wetting his cheeks. He murmured garbled words, stroking her hair and closing his eyes.

Helena and Andy glanced at each other.

One visit down, one to go.

Clara Banks' mother took the news much the same way, but her father railed, shouting about Clara staying over at Shona's house, so what the hell was going on? Helena shook her head at the old teenage trick—both pretending they were elsewhere, when really they'd planned to…what? Stay outside? At Stephan's? The latter seemed unlikely, given that Stephan wasn't even supposed to have gone out. Another friend's place?

"Mrs Long thought Shona was staying here," Helena said, steeling herself for him to explode.

"The stupid pair of buggers," he said, drawing away from his wife on the sofa to pace the room. "So what are you saying, they planned to kill themselves and chose tonight to do it? They jumped?"

"No. Early indications show they were pushed from behind."

"Pardon me?" he bellowed, his cheeks flaring bright red. "Pissing hell. Who would want to do that to two girls?"

"That's what we need to find out." As she had with Mr and Mrs Long once they'd calmed down, she asked, "Do you know of anyone who would want to harm your daughter, Mr Bates?"

"Absolutely bloody not!"

With a few more questions asked, and Mr Bates assuring them that no, they didn't need a fucking FLO, Helena and Andy left the house and headed back to the station.

Louise had to leave the front desk to go to the toilet, so she took the chance while all was quiet. When she came back, she could have kicked herself. A folded piece of paper was on the mat, rippled and slightly damp in places. She unlocked the door and rushed outside, but of course, no one was there.

Behind the desk, she fished out some gloves and snapped them on, then picked up the note. It stuck together where the author had used glue for the cut-out letters, but the words were as plain as day: *Forty-eight hours from the time Stephan disappeared, he will emerge from his cocoon, new, baptised, and a willing disciple. Godspeed.*

"What the fuck?" she whispered, getting out an evidence bag and slipping the letter inside. Then she accessed the CCTV to see what showed up. A shape like before — the same man, obviously.

Helena was going to bloody kill her when she found out Louise had left the desk unmanned.

Shit.

She sent Helena a message rather then tell her verbally. The reply had her hating herself even more: *WTF, Louise?*

CHAPTER FIFTEEN

He rushed through the streets, keeping to the residential areas where there was no CCTV. Making it home without seeing a soul, he stepped inside, wobbly from all the blood of Christ he'd imbibed, not to mention the adrenaline lending a hand. He locked up with shaking fingers, then took a moment to calm down.

What have you done?

His teen self had asked that, and he didn't have an adequate answer, so he walked down into the cellar to check on his project.

The lad was asleep, curled up in the foetal position, sucking his thumb. That must be a leftover habit remaining from childhood — or perhaps his mind had prompted him to suck it through fear. Stephan needed comfort.

He stared down at him, at the ratty grey blanket, the sleeve hem of the green robe poking out near the boy's face. This was a child, and he shouldn't be doing this to him, putting him through what he himself had hated at the same age.

What is wrong with me?

He struggled with his teenage self who insisted on pushing to the fore, coming in to defend this other kid. Shoving him back wasn't easy, and the Devil took his place, laughing and saying he should just kill the figure on the mattress and be done with it—Stephan wouldn't comply, no matter how long he was held captive.

He didn't know what to do for the best. Stephan had seen his face on the cliff top, albeit in darkness, but what if he'd got a good look in the moonlight? What if he could identify him later down the line if he let him go?

"Then you keep him here forever," Grandmother said, folding her arms over her ample bosom. "Teach him the ways of God yourself instead of taking him to church."

"That's contradicting what you said. I thought he had to go to church?"

"I can change the rules if I want to."

"Oh, go away."

She blew a raspberry. "That's not a very nice thing to say to me. Remember who you're speaking to."

"My tormenter," he said. "The one who made me this way."

"You keep blaming me, but in the end, it was your own will that placed you on this path."

"It wasn't. It was fear — of you."

"And are you still scared of me?"

He wouldn't tell her yes. She'd love that. "No. You need to go back to Hell, where you belong."

She disappeared, leaving him with the Devil standing on one side, his teen on the other, his third self in the middle. Neither of those two would steer him in the right direction. But what *was* the right way?

Killing Stephan?

Setting him free?

Releasing him but still forcing him to embrace the Lord?

"I don't know what to do," he said, kneeling beside the mattress. He stroked Stephan's hair, hoping that somehow, the lad would think it was his mother.

His brain shorted out, and he whipped his hand away.

"No. I won't touch you. Won't be kind to you. I suffered, so you'll suffer."

He thundered up the stairs and slammed the door, locking it, then hurried into the kitchen, grabbing the bottle of Jesus' blood. He swallowed a good few gulps, his saviour infusing him, sending him into a calmer state. Everyone argued in his head, and he paced, trying to block them out.

"My main aim is to bring another to the flock." He muttered that over and over until the sound of *their* voices grew faint.

He was going mad. Had to be if he could hear people talking when they weren't even there.

"The world is a dark place," Mum said, shoving her hands into the pocket of her apron and drawing out a can of polish and a yellow cloth dirtied with lines of dust.

It was the summer holidays, and he sat watching her work in Mrs Fotheringale's house, cleaning up for a rich woman as ungrateful as Grandmother. Mum did this for a living and had a huge bunch of keys on a big circle of steel, each key belonging to someone who either didn't have time to clean their own houses or couldn't, for whatever reason. Grandmother's reason was laziness – she had all day, every day, to do it herself. She didn't employ Mum, though. That would seem 'too strange' to outsiders, and Grandmother couldn't be seen as being strange.

Even though she was.

"You can't trust anyone these days," Mum went on, shaking the polish can. "Which is why you have

to come with me until you're old enough to stay at home by yourself."

"When will that be?" he asked.

"Oh, I don't know. Thirty?"

"Thirty!"

Mum laughed, throwing her head back, and he knew she was joking then.

"Perhaps thirteen," she said.

That was only two more years, and if it meant going to work with Mum while he wasn't in school instead of having Grandmother watching him, he'd suffer through the boredom.

Mrs Fotheringale had some lovely things, like golden mantel clocks and silver trays – real silver, so Mum had said. The lady was rich and no mistake, and he had to be careful in this house. No running about where he might accidentally knock something off a sideboard and smash it. No noise – Mr Fotheringale was always in bed, never seeming to be out of it. Mum said he was poorly and wouldn't be long in karking it. She didn't have to clean his bedroom.

Good. He wasn't sure he'd want to see a half-dead bloke propped up against the pillows, smelly because he couldn't get in the bath.

Grandmother was good friends with Mrs Fotheringale. They chatted at church on the occasions Grandmother took him along, and he listened to them nattering about so-and-so here and so-and-so there.

Gossips, Mum called them.

159

"Why does Grandmother have so much money?" he asked Mum.

She rubbed at a stubborn spot on the glass door of a display cabinet. "Because she married a rich man."

"So she didn't go to work and earn it?"

"No." Mum seemed to find the glass particularly interesting.

"Why didn't Dad like her?"

"Your dad didn't like her because...he had a difficult upbringing and had to do things he didn't want to do." She paused, turning to look at him, her face going white. "Listen to me. If she asks you to follow God and Jesus, and you don't want to, you'll tell me, won't you?"

He nodded. Of course he would. He'd do anything for Mum.

He wondered why she'd said that. He opened his mouth to ask her, but she cut him off.

"Now, enough. Let's stop yakking so I can finish here, then we can go and get some ice cream from the parlour in town. I can stretch to that, and we deserve a treat."

Maybe one day he'd find out what had happened in Dad's life, but for now, he snapped his mouth shut. Good job he did, because Mrs Fotheringale was back, calling out from the hallway. Mum would need to hurry up now the lady of the house was home.

He hated people like her.

It was going to be a tedious summer.

160

He woke with his cheek pressed against the kitchen table, drool dribbling. He swiped at it and blinked. Daylight streamed around the edges of the curtains, trying to penetrate the thin material. What time of day was it? Morning? Afternoon? He'd swallowed enough blood to knock him out for hours, so he wouldn't be surprised if it was well past noon.

Squinting at the clock, he tried to make out where the hands pointed. It could be ten past nine or quarter to two. He pushed himself standing and trudged upstairs, eager to wash away the grimy feeling alcohol always brought. Under the spray, he strained to listen.

No voices in his head.

Relaxed now he was safe from *them*, he washed then dried himself, thinking of the child in the tree. Children. There had been so many. Grandmother, Dad, him, Jayden. Were there more he didn't know about? Would he put someone else in there if it didn't work out with Stephan?

"You were supposed to use the same child for both the tree *and* the cellar, you dense imbecile," Grandmother said.

He jumped and covered his private parts with the towel. "Get out!"

"You've got nothing I haven't seen before," she said. "I don't think it will be enough for

161

Stephan. The cellar, I mean. Look at how long it took *you* to obey. Several incarcerations in both places. You were such a difficult child." She sighed as though everything was a trial. Any second now, she'd claim she needed a fainting couch, the dramatic bitch.

Why did she have to keep bringing that up, like he was some kind of slow coach who hadn't accepted what she'd wanted at first?

He hated her.

She glided through the door, and he stared at it, pressing a palm on the surface. It was solid, so how had she just walked into it like that? Anger and confusion set up a battle inside him, and he stalked out into his bedroom where he threw on clothes, his movements jerky.

A hurried breakfast later—he only had time for a bowl of Weetabix—he opened the cellar door, the balaclava firmly in place. The smell of urine hit him, and he reckoned Stephan had used the bucket. Downstairs, he watched from the newel post. The scary Jesus picture studied them both.

Stephan was awake, sitting up, knees bent, and he hugged his legs—pretending it was his mother he embraced?

I remember it well.

"Let me go home," Stephan said, all surly and as if he had the right to say such a thing. "The police will be looking for me, you know."

"No, they won't. I sent them a letter. They'll wait until tomorrow."

"Tomorrow?" The lad groaned and rested his forehead on his knees.

"Yes, that's when you'll be ready."

"Ready for what?" The words were muffled. The kid was annoyed. Belligerent. A typical teen.

"Jesus."

Stephan's head snapped up. "Fuck you and your Jesus shit!" he shouted, eyes bulging, neck cords straining, pronounced.

"Language." He stopped himself from whacking a hand over his mouth. Grandmother's word coming out of him wasn't right. "Count yourself lucky you're not in the hollow just yet."

"What?" Stephan frowned.

"There's a cross there, and you could be hanging off it right at this moment, but you're not, you're here, so be grateful."

"A cross?" The boy's words croaked.

"Like the one used for the man who died for us."

"Fuck's sake..."

He sighed, weary of Stephan's attitude. It reminded him so much of his own at that age. He could kind of understand why Grandmother had got so angry with him. "You need to calm down. I will get the crow and read to you. That should help."

"I don't want to hear anything from that bloody crow."

Stephan was going to be more difficult than he'd thought.

"Slap him," the Devil said.

"Kill him and start again," Grandmother put in.

"Please, just let him go home," his teen whined.

"No to any of it," he said, chopping at the air with his hand, bringing an end to the matter.

"What?" Stephan frowned.

"Nothing." He stomped upstairs and collected the crow from the kitchen table, the wings smooth and shiny from so much use. Back in the cellar, he sat cross-legged outside the perimeter and opened the book at random. "'*For I know the plans I have for you,*' declares the Lord, '*plans to prosper you and not to harm you, plans to give you hope and a future.*' Isn't that what you want, Stephan? To have the Lord looking out for you like He promises?"

"How can bloody God do that? He doesn't exist, you twat."

The boy was so far away from goodness it was unreal.

"Be quiet." He selected another page. "'*For God so loved the world that he gave his one and only*

164

Son, that whoever believes in Him shall not perish but have eternal life.' Do you understand that, boy?"

"Just bloody well knob off, will you?" Stephan rested on his side and hid his head beneath the grey blanket.

"He's not going to learn," Grandmother said. "Get rid of him. Find another one."

What did she mean?

"Stop being coy," she snapped, sitting beside him. "You know what I meant."

He couldn't do it right now. It was daylight.

"Yes, you can. No one will see you," she encouraged. "Look where the house is."

"But people will see from their windows along this road, and those people on the estate could look out," he said.

"Who are you talking to?" Stephan asked.

"No one," he said and thought about the task ahead.

She was right. Stephan wouldn't work. He was too headstrong to want to change his way of thinking.

"Do it right this time," Grandmother said. "First put the new child in the tree, *then* down here. I should have known you'd mess it all up."

She got up and waltzed somewhere behind him.

He blew out a heavy breath. Why couldn't she just leave him alone?

165

If the police had found those girls he'd pushed, and they knew Stephan was missing, would they still be there?

He had to chance it.

An hour later, no police in sight, they stood on the cliff top, Stephan minus the robe and slippers. They were needed for the new boy. He'd put a blindfold on the kid and decided that if the Lord wanted Stephan to return home, he would guide the unseeing boy to safety. He'd tied his hands behind his back so he couldn't take the shield off his face.

It was God's decision.

"So you don't have to take any blame?" Grandmother asked, the wind coming in off the sea and wafting through her hair. It blew in all directions, slapping her in the face then streaking out behind her.

"It wasn't my fault Jayden died, and it won't be if Stephan does," he said.

"What?" the kid asked, shaking.

"I'm speaking to someone else," he said. "Not you."

Stephan frowned. He was shitting bricks. Someone else was there with them? Who? Some other mad bloke? They had to be near the sea — the damn stuff whooshed nearby. From walking

166

to this spot, he sensed they were on grass, so he reckoned they were on the cliff top. Was he going to fall off like Shona and Clara?

He couldn't stop shaking.

I just want my mum.

"God will determine what happens," the crackpot said. "Goodbye, Stephan."

The bloke was walking away, going by the shuffle of footsteps. Definitely grass then. The rope around Stephan's wrists burned, and he was petrified of moving. What if he sat on the ground and it tipped him over a ledge? What if he moved one step and it did the same? He'd be better off keeping still. Someone would come along, wouldn't they? People walked their dogs up here all the time — providing he was where he thought he was.

The man must have gone, as all the noise that remained was Stephan's ragged breathing, his staggered heartbeat, and the crash and slap of the waves.

He stood there for ages, his legs going to sleep, his shoulders hurting from the position his arms were in. Although the sun was out, it wasn't particularly warm, and his clothes weren't doing anything to keep him cosy.

A distant bark — *fucking hell, someone's coming!* — and Stephan called out.

"Help! Help me!"

"What the sodding hell's going on here?" a man asked.

"Help me," Stephan managed, trembling all over, worried shitless if he moved his foot he'd go down into the waves.

Something nudged him, and dampness seeped through his trousers at the knee. Snuffles. Another bark, then a yip.

"Scoundrel, stop bothering the poor lad," the man said. "Sit!"

The blindfold was removed, and sunshine poured onto Stephan's face. He shut his eyes — the light was too much — and struggled to keep his breathing even.

"Dear God, you're tied up. Sit down on the grass here, kid."

Stephan shook his head. What if it was the Jesus bloke pretending to be someone else? "No. I can't…" He opened his eyes, waiting for them to adjust.

And there he was, on the cliff top, but far away from it, just outside the tree line of the woods. He sank to his knees and sobbed, the dog, a yellow Labrador, jumping all over him, eager to lick his face.

Stephan cried.

CHAPTER SIXTEEN

Helena jammed her phone to her ear. "Yep?" What a bloody frustrating night and day they'd had so far.

Helena and her team had managed about four hours of sleep when they'd all gone home about three in the morning, then they were back in the incident room for eight. Whatever lines of enquiry they'd tried today had all come to dead ends. House-to-house was in action on the estate opposite the cliff top where the girls had gone over, but no one had seen anything. Officers would be going back there later, after work, to talk to the people who hadn't been in.

"Looks like Stephan's been found," Louise said.

Helena's heart skipped a few beats. "Where?"

"On the cliff top. Alive."

All the strength drained out of Helena, and she slumped in her office chair. "Oh, thank God. Who found him?"

"Some old bloke walking his dog. Officers rang it in."

"Me and Andy will leave right away. Thanks."

She stuffed her phone in her pocket and ran to the incident room. "Guys, Stephan's been found alive. He's on the cliff top. Ol, get hold of Dave—he's at the Korby's house, went back there this morning. Tell him where Stephan is but not to let the parents know yet. Last thing we need is them traipsing down there."

"Okay, guv."

"Andy, we're off." Helena trounced out and down the stairs, waiting for him in the car.

He got in, and she drove away, a rush of relief winging through her body, sending her limbs heavy.

"Another one let go early," Andy said. "What's the point? Are we missing something?"

Helena swerved around a corner. "Only that the abductor can't stick to his or her word, so they're not as organised as they might think."

"First-time job?" he asked, glancing to look out of his window.

"Probably. He's not planned it enough, obviously." She thought about the CCTV from last night, where it showed the same figure from the first time they'd posted a note, and again, no face visible. "All that time it takes to make those notes, and they don't follow through with what they've said?"

"I still say Jayden's death was a mistake now Zach's confirmed an asthma attack brought on by cold, panic, and mould spores." Andy leant his elbow on the door. "Would this dickhead have kept Jayden had he not died?"

"I'm inclined to believe so, but we'll never know, will we? Jayden isn't here to tell us what went on, and at this rate, I'm beginning to believe we'll never find who's doing this."

"Think positive," Andy said.

At the top of the cliff, just past the estate, she drove straight onto the grass towards a police car already parked, a huddle of people, and a dog lying curled up. She stopped close by and got out, rushing to the group. Stephan sat on the grass, his wrists sore, just like Jayden's had been.

Crouching, she said, "Stephan Korby?"

He nodded, eyes watery, a vivid bruise on his cheekbone.

"Thank God for that." She smiled gently.

"Don't talk to me about God."

What? "I'm Detective Inspector Helena Stratton, but please call me Helena." She showed him her ID. "And this is Detective Sergeant Mald, but he's known as Andy, all right? We're going to take you to the station and get you seen by a doctor."

"I just want my mum," he said, his dry lips quivering.

"I know, love, and you will. Andy, will you settle Stephan in the car while I talk to this gentleman, please?"

Helena stood, and Andy helped Stephan to do the same. They walked off together, Stephan appearing stiff and cold.

"There's a foil blanket in the boot," she called.

Andy raised a hand in acknowledgement.

Helena turned her attention to the man. "I appreciate that these officers here might already have asked you questions, but can you quickly go through what happened for me?"

About sixty, with tufty grey hair and weathered features, he nodded, sucking in his bottom lip.

"What's your name, sir?" she asked.

"Reg Armitage. I live on that estate there. Gave my address to these two." He jabbed his thumb at the uniforms.

"That's great. So were you just walking your dog?" she asked.

"Dunno what else you think I'd be bleedin' doing." He sighed. "Sorry, this has been a bit of a shock, know what I mean?"

"I can imagine. So…"

"Well, I came out of the woods, right here, actually, but before I got this far, I saw that lad just there." He pointed to a spot a couple of metres along. "He was facing the sea, so I got a good look at the fact he had rope around his wrists, which had been tied behind his back. Bloody shocking, that is. Well, to begin with, I thought it was one of those cheeky sex games that seem all the rage these days—you can't watch telly without that bondage business cropping up, can you?"

Helena bit back a smile at 'cropping'. "No. Carry on."

One of the officers coughed and turned away to pet the dog.

"Anyway," Reg said, "Scoundrel here—that's my dog; bit obvious how he got his name, although he's behaving himself fine enough now. What was I saying?" He scratched his head. "Ah, yes. Scoundrel barked and ran off ahead, going up to the lad and pressing his damn nose on his trousers. He's always doing that, drives my wife batty—then again, she's batty enough as it is so…" He stared around as though forgetting where he was. "Right. So I walked up to this spot here and saw it was a lad. He had a blindfold on, so that reinforced the bondage thing in my head, and I took it off, but

173

it was a *child*. Surely they can't be getting up to that sort of thing at his age, can they?"

"No, Reg." God, Helena loved this bloke. "Stephan was abducted from here yesterday."

"Abducted, you say? Blimey…" His eyes watered, and he cleared his throat. "You'd best be getting him back to his mum then, hadn't you? I've got to nip to the shop now—Vera wants a pint of blue top and a bar of Milka, the sort with nuts in, but I'll be back home after that if you need to talk to me again."

"Are you really all right, though, Reg?" she asked.

"Don't you fret. Scoundrel will look after me."

The dog currently lapped up the officer's attention, squirming on his back and splaying his back legs, tail flapping. He didn't seem like he'd look after anyone, let alone Reg.

Helena smiled. "All right then. Thank you for calling us."

"Oh, I didn't," Reg said. "I was surprised to see a police car turn up, I can tell you. I don't have my phone on me and was wondering what to do, and the boy didn't have his phone either."

Helena's mouth hung open. Someone else must have done it. Had the abductor been hiding in the woods, watching? Why ring the bloody police if it meant he might get caught?

Or did he enjoy sailing close to the wind, keeping an eye on things from a distance?

She glanced at the officers. "Get in those woods and do a search. I'll ring for more help." Torn with what to do—stay and keep an eye out or get Stephan back to the station—she thanked Reg again then headed for the car while the uniforms disappeared into the woods. Opening the door, she stuck her head inside.

"Can you stay here until reinforcements arrive?" she asked Andy.

He stepped out of the vehicle and came to her side. She smiled at a worried-looking Stephan then closed the door.

"The old boy wasn't the one to phone the bloody police," she said. "So I've sent the other two into the woods to see if they spot anyone or anything."

"Crikey. Do you think the abductor did it? Don't answer that. I'll ring the station now for more uniforms. I'll hang about here until they arrive, then go in and help them."

"Thanks. I really think this poor kid needs to see his mother as soon as possible, otherwise I'd stay."

"No problem. I'll get a lift back with one of the others."

She nodded and hopped into the driver's seat, glancing at Stephan in the rearview mirror. "Okay, love?"

He nodded. "It was a man who took me. Shona and Clara jumped off the cliff, and he punched me, then I woke up in a basement."

Brilliant information. There weren't many houses around here that had them. "Two seconds." She rang Ol. "Look up houses with basements or cellars for me. I'm just coming back in now."

She propped her phone in the drink holder between the front seats then drove away.

"Want to talk about it?" Helena asked him.

"Yeah. I'm all right now I'm safe." He took a deep breath, and it came out shuddery. "He had a balaclava on in the house but not on the cliff last night. Was it last night? I don't know how long I've been gone."

"Yes, it was. Did you see his face clearly?"

"It was dark, but there was a moon. I think his face was fat, like he had puffy cheeks."

Finally, a description. "Okay. Anything else?"

"A big nose. Oh, and when I saw him with the balaclava on, he had weird eyes, like they were piggy, and his lips were fat and all."

"That's excellent, Stephan. Can you remember what colour his eyes were?"

"Black, or they looked like they were. I couldn't see much because I was on a mattress, chained to the wall, and he sat on the floor opposite, a bit away from me. There was a brass lamp, some old-fashioned thing, but it wasn't very bright. He put me in this dress…"

Helena's heart jolted at that, and chills spread all over her. "A dress?"

"Not like a woman's or anything. Might have been sack material, green, and it itched."

"This might be a hard question, but did you have to take your clothes off and put it on?" It might explain why Jayden had been found in only his socks and boxers.

"No, I woke up with it on over my clothes. It had a rope belt. And my shoes had been taken off. I had old-man slippers on with green wire wrapped around them."

What the hell? "Can you describe the basement?"

"Loads of boxes, a wine rack, but that wasn't dusty or anything like the other stuff. It had a sign above it, saying something about Jesus' blood. There were crates. Blue. One had a teapot in it, and another had a feather duster sticking out. And there was a creepy picture on the wall. Of Jesus. The man kept reading from the Bible — he called it 'the crow', and he just wouldn't shut up. I had to stay awake until Jesus told him to stop reading."

So there *was* a religious angle.

"Do you remember what he read?"

"Only some of it. He said it was Corinthian, something like that. Gongs and cymbals, I remember those."

What do they mean? "We're here now, so let's get you inside. I'll ring your parents while we wait for the doctor, okay? Would you like to speak to your mum on the phone?" She parked and caught sight of Stephan in the mirror.

Tears streaked his face. "What about Shona and Clara?"

"There's time enough for that, love. Let's take one step at a time, eh?"

"The girls are dead, aren't they?"

Helena twisted to look at him. "It's too much to take in after what you've been through. I have a duty to get you seen by a doctor first and not cause you too much distress. We can talk some more after, all right?"

"I'll take that as a yes then."

She grabbed her phone from the drink holder, got out, and helped him do the same, the foil blanket rustling with his movements. After locking the car, she led him into the station. Louise's face lit up from behind the desk.

"Soft interview room," Helena said. "And call the duty doctor, please. I'll deal with Mr and Mrs Korby. Can you bring a sandwich and a hot, sweet tea?"

She took him to the room with the sofas and, while he sat, she rang his mother, who screamed. Martin came on the line.

"What's happened?" he asked, sounding panicked and out of breath. "Dave said Stephan was okay. Why's she screaming?"

"Everything's fine," Helena said. "I think Julie just got overwhelmed to know I'm with Stephan now. I have him at the station. He's alive, like Dave told you. We're just waiting for the doctor, then you can see him."

"Is he all right?"

"I'll pass you over." She handed the phone to Stephan.

He took it, crying, and listened to his dad, nodding and sobbing.

Someone knocked on the door, so Helena got up to answer it. Louise stood on the other side, holding a prepacked sandwich and a cup of tea on a scratched, plastic tray.

"I legged it to the shop on the corner," she said. "The bloody food vending machine people didn't come to refill it yet."

"Thanks." Helena leant forward and whispered, "Is the video recording?"

"Yes."

"Cheers." She took the tray and closed the door. She placed the tea and sandwich on the table.

Stephan finished on the phone and handed it back to her. She ended the call with his father then sat on one of the chairs.

"Get some food in you," she said. "You must be starving."

He opened the package and took out half a ham and cheese, white bread.

"Feel better now you've spoken to your dad?"

He bit into the sandwich and nodded.

"I bet. While you're eating, I'll ask you questions where you only need to nod or shake your head. Is that okay with you?"

He nodded.

"I'll just call for an appropriate adult, a witness — I'm not allowed to speak to you without one." She rang the front desk.

A uniform came in and stood beside the door.

"So," she said, "do you think the man meant you any harm?"

Head shake.

"Do you know if anyone else was in that house?"

Head shake.

"When he took you out of the house, did you already have the blindfold on?"

He swallowed his bite of food. "Not until just before we left."

"Did you manage to look out of any windows to see where you might be? A street, perhaps?"

"No, the curtains were all shut, but the room he took me in after the cellar was what he called the 'drawing room', then he told his gran off, but she wasn't even there."

"I see." *An invisible gran?* "What did he say to her?"

"He swore."

"It's fine, you can tell me."

"He said: *Fuck off, you old bitch. I will not kill him. What did I do to deserve a grandmother like you, eh?*"

So someone was telling the abductor what to do? Through an earpiece maybe? Or was it schizophrenia? With him saying he wouldn't kill, it sounded more and more like he'd panicked when Jayden had died so had left him at the park.

Stephan sipped some tea. "Sometimes, it was like he was talking to himself." Picking up the other half of the sandwich, he chomped on it.

"You just eat that now. We'll talk when you're finished. Excuse me for a moment while I make a call."

She left the room and rang Ol. "Anything?"

"There are seventeen houses with cellars," she said. "All of them are detached and in their own grounds. What would you like me to do?"

"Take Evan or Phil and go visiting; actually, go with uniforms as well. I can't really talk right now, so use your initiative. Mainly see if anyone acts suspicious."

"Okay. Are you with Stephan?"

"Yes—well, outside the soft room."

"Is he okay?"

"Should be."

"I'll leave you be. Hopefully we won't be long. All the houses are in the same area."

"Where?"

"They sort of branch off from the estate on the cliff top—you know the ones? I had a look on the map, and the park where Jayden was found is on the other side of the woods to that estate."

"Interesting."

The doctor strode down the corridor.

"I have to go," Helena said.

She showed him into the room where Stephan sat.

Time to get the lad checked out, then he'd have to be questioned again.

Poor sod.

"There was a school uniform, shoes, and a Nike backpack under the stairs in the basement," Stephan said, as though there hadn't been a break in conversation.

Jayden's things? Dear God...

182

CHAPTER SEVENTEEN

He'd watched that old man approach Stephan, and relief had gone through him that God had listened and He wasn't just some imaginary being. Why else would the man have turned up if it wasn't God directing him?

"He was just walking his dog, stupid," his teen side said.

He ignored him and drank some of Jesus' blood—he was relying on it a bit too much lately, but needs must.

His mind wandered to what he must do now. Tonight. Another boy.

Could he do it for a third time? Four answers came back. Three of them were from his self that he was right now, Grandmother, and the Devil.

Yes. The no was from his teen side. All the rage that had carried him through recent years had convinced him that this mission to bring youngsters into the fold was the right thing to do. He'd wanted other boys to suffer—why should it just be him? He hadn't bargained on feeling guilty, though. Seeing Jayden in the tree and Stephan in the cellar...it had brought back his own feelings of insecurity and fear, of wanting Mum, wishing his captor, the supposedly Catholic grandmother, would set him free. Those lads must have thought the same about him.

More and more these past couple of days, he was leaning towards ignoring what Grandmother wanted. What about God? And Jesus? Would they want him snatching kids away and hiding them in terrible places?

No.

"If you don't do it, I'll put *you* in the tree," Grandmother said.

That scared him. He didn't want to go back there.

"Okay, I'll do it just this once more," he said.

Grandmother stole his Jesus blood goblet and drank the lot.

She needed to watch herself. If she wasn't careful, he'd snap like he did before, and then she'd have it reconfirmed he wasn't a pushover.

Grandmother sat on the chaise in the drawing room and gazed out of the window. She was ignoring him because he'd refused to go around people's houses, knocking on doors and handing out church leaflets. Why was she so manic about it? All the other parishioners just sat through the service, then went home and lived life like everyone else. How come Grandmother needed to spread the word to anyone and everyone?

Father Pinto had said to just go along to appease her. She paid a lot of money into the church coffers, and Father didn't want to lose her, not when a hole in the roof needed fixing, so nodding and doing as you were told was best.

The advice was sound. After all, since he'd been in the hollow and the cellar, his mind was no longer his own. Grandmother told him what to think, what to eat, what to say.

He was getting sick of it, especially since he'd been hearing other people speaking in his head lately. It scared him. Only mad people heard voices, didn't they?

"I just don't feel pushing our beliefs onto people is the best way to go about it," he said. "Why not make flyers for the summer fete instead? That way, people can come along and see us of their own accord. Wouldn't you prefer it if—"

"Oh, shut your fat mouth, porky," she said.

"If you were a true believer, you wouldn't call me those names." That wasn't him. That was one of the voices who'd said that.

"If you were a true believer, you wouldn't question me at every turn," she snapped. "Go and whip yourself. Ten lashes."

He didn't like doing that. It hurt so badly, and she always put TCP on the welts afterwards, and they stung and burned, as though his skin had caught fire.

"No," he said.

She turned from the window and stared at him, her mouth hanging open. "No?"

"No."

"Why, you wretched little pig. Get down in that cellar." She pointed at the door.

"No."

Up she got, rage sending her face into a spiteful mask, and he got up, too, backing away from her. He reached the door, and she advanced, eyes bulging, spittle dribbling. At the cellar door, he automatically opened it, years of training prompting him to do as she said even though he didn't want to. He stood with his back pressed against it, and she came closer, pointing a wobbling finger at the stairs.

"Get down them," she said.

"No."

She lunged at him then, but he side-stepped, and she crashed into the door, skewing to the right, towards the gaping black rectangle of the opening. Part of him wanted to reach out and grab her, but the other pinned his arms to his sides, and she sailed midair for a moment, then thudded onto the steps, tumbling, tumbling, tumbling.

He went upstairs and sat on a spare room bed for an hour, watching a game show. Then he called for an ambulance, saying Grandmother must have fallen while he'd been in the room. "Please, help me, she's all I have left."

This new self said this, but his teen side laughed and laughed.

"Why did you have to think of that?" Grandmother asked.

He shrugged.

The hours since he'd let Stephan go had sped by so quickly. He wanted it to be daytime forever, so he didn't have to go out there and claim another child for the hollow.

"If you do as I say, it'll all stop." She sniffed.

Would it? Should he give it a try?

"It's getting dark," she said. "You know what to do."

Matty Vines pedalled faster. If he got all his papers delivered quickly, he could make it home in time to watch the catch-up version of *Tipping Point* with Mum. Mind you, he didn't have that many papers to do these days. People just didn't buy the real thing when the internet could tell you all you needed to know. The houses he went to were mainly old folks, and he just had two more to visit, then he could get home.

He took a shortcut through the park, even though Mum had told him not to go there since Jayden Rook had been found dead. And she'd said to avoid the woods for now, plus the cliff top. News had spread that Shona Long and Clara Bates had fallen off the cliff, plus Stephan had been nabbed by some weird bloke. Matty couldn't get over it. All those kids were in his year at school, in some of his classes, even.

He bit his lip upon approaching the tree line in the park. Should he go through there? It wouldn't take a minute, whereas going the long way would mean fifteen.

Sod it. Mum would never know.

He flicked his headlamp to a higher beam — Dad had bought it for Christmas. The woods lit up quite far ahead, plus a fair stretch either side. Matty would spot anything coming, and it'd give him ample time to turn back and go the other way. But nothing untoward happened, and he made it to the other side unscathed.

Mums. They always worried too much.

Keeping his lamp on high, he sped over the cliff top grass, avoiding the estate because the houses he wanted were at the other end, about half a mile out. He'd more than likely get bullied or whatever by the estate kids, so he was better off taking this route.

There. He'd made it, safe and sound. He was getting older now, would soon be a man, so he needed to make decisions like this by himself. He pulled up outside a great big posh place at the end of the line of houses, white with black beams on the outer walls, like something from Tudor times. He'd seen these types of buildings in history lessons, and apart from not having a thatched roof, this one was just the same. Mum reckoned you had to earn a packet to live there.

He got off the bike. Walking up the drive — because the owner had a go at him once for leaving tyre tracks in the gravel; the homeowners here were all weird about that — he caught sight of people at the open door, peachy light spilling out onto the front step and the shoes of two police officers. Matty's heart pattered harder. Why did it always do that whenever he saw a copper, even if he hadn't done anything wrong?

Mrs Zadolka, some foreign woman, held her wrinkly, skinny hand out for the paper. Matty passed it over, raring to get off, but the policemen turned to look at him, pinning him with their stares, so he stayed rooted to the spot.

"Have you got much more delivering to do?" one of them asked.

He seemed kind, like maybe he'd done a paper round as a kid.

"Just one more," Matty said, smiling.

"Well, make sure you get home sharpish. You really shouldn't be out when it's dark at the moment."

"Okay," Matty said, remembering his school friends and what had happened to them.

"Yes, boys going missing left and right," Mrs Zadolka added, nodding, her nose like a raven's beak. "About your age, too, Matty. Or so I've heard."

A shiver trickled down Matty's back, seeming to pop at the bottom then spread into a million goosebumps. Maybe he ought to go home the long way, not through the woods this time. A part of him wanted the police to come with him to the next house, but they had better things to do, didn't they?

Instead, he turned and strode away, his legs shaking a bit. It *was* dark, and boys *had* gone missing. It was a scary thought.

"So no one is in next door?" Mrs Zadolka asked, her voice carrying.

"Not that we could see," the kind policeman replied. "Two detectives are at the bottom of the road, working their way up, asking questions."

"I wouldn't know if he's there or not," she said. "I can't see his front door from my house."

Matty sped up until he reached his bike, then climbed on it. He'd got the willies from what Mrs Zadolka had said and wanted to shove the last paper through that weird man's door then race home. Or he could ditch the paper and pretend he'd posted it.

No, that would be too much guilt. He wouldn't want to lie to his boss, the jolly Mr Pickles, although why people called him that when his name was Rogerson, Matty didn't know.

He rode off, headlight beam bouncing each time he went over a pebble or down a dip in the pavement. It took about a minute to get to the house, and he cycled up the drive—the bloke didn't complain about tyre tracks here. As he neared the front door, he frowned, heart seeming to lodge itself in his throat. He swallowed, telling himself to calm down, but he didn't know what to do in this sort of situation.

The man was on the ground, curled up on his side, like he'd fallen and hurt himself. What if he was dead? What if he was unconscious and Matty couldn't wake him up? Should he go back and get those coppers?

His stomach knotted, and he felt a bit sick. Off the bike, he let it fall where it may and raced towards the prone figure.

"Are you all right, Mr Keffler? The police are just down the road. I'll go and get them."

"No," Mr Keffler gasped out. "I was chasing my daft dog. He's hurt his leg. Don't worry about me. Go in and see if he's okay, will you?"

Matty stared at the door. It stood ajar, but no lights were on inside. The place had always given him the creeps, as well as the owner, so to go in there was asking a bit much. "I'll ring for help instead." He tugged his phone out of his pocket.

"No, please. Just go and find my puppy. I haven't had him long, and he'll be scared."

Matty knew he shouldn't stay, but he couldn't very well just leave this bloke on the ground, could he? And what about the poor dog?

God...

He'd be quick.

He stepped inside, patting the wall for a light switch. Not finding one, he took a few more steps, feeling a right wally for calling, "Here, doggy! Are you okay?"

Light came from behind, and a *click-click-click*, similar to the noise his bike made when he rode it slowly.

The door snapped shut, and Matty spun round to see if the wind had done it. A bright light speared the darkness — *my headlight!* — and he rushed forward to grab his bicycle off Mr Keffler and get the hell out.

"No," the weirdo man said gruffly. "You're staying here with me. God and Jesus want to meet you."

CHAPTER EIGHTEEN

Helena was about to head home. The day had been frustrating and sad in many respects, and although she'd dearly love to keep going, she unfortunately couldn't run on gas. Tiredness was creeping up on her, and no amount of coffee could fix it. Unless she had a burst of adrenaline, she wouldn't function on all cylinders for much longer.

She propped her arse on the edge of a spare desk in the incident room and pressed her hands on it, leaning back. Her whole body ached, and her feet were throbbing, the sons of bitches.

"Let's chat about the latest before we leave," Helena said. "Ol?"

"Okay, the drivers caught on CCTV... We spoke to them. All of them seemed legit. The houses with basements — all the residents were in except for one. No one appeared strange or gave off any dodgy vibes. I know that doesn't mean anything, but they were all too frail, in my opinion. The uniforms said the same about the people they spoke to. I honestly can't see these folks being strong enough to kidnap teenage boys."

"I feel the same," Evan said. "The man who wasn't in, that's a Mr Keffler. When we got back here, I looked him up to find out where he works. I thought he could be there — Lenton's Carpentry and Joinery, by the way — so I gave them a ring. He's got a week off, so maybe he's gone away for a few days."

"It's possible. Did you check airports and whatnot, just to be on the safe side?"

"Yes." Evan nodded. "He hasn't left the country. My next step was to get his credit and debit cards checked so we can see where he's spent his money recently, but, as usual, we're on hold with that. The banks want us to go through the proper channels, so...paperwork first, then they'll divulge. That's on the backburner until tomorrow or the day after, depending on how fast we can get things moving and how quickly they then respond."

"Christ." Helena pushed her knuckles on her temples. She hated it when they came across legalities and couldn't just muscle information out of people. It held them back, and in the meantime, criminals were left to carry on with whatever the hell they were doing. "You'd think with it being kids going missing and turning up dead, they'd be a bit more sympathetic."

"Yeah," Phil said, "but innocent until proven guilty and all that. No way can they dish out private stuff willy-nilly, just because some fella hasn't opened his door and we're hoping it's him."

"I know, I know." Helena sighed. "And it might not even *be* him, but Stephan was certain it was a basement. He remembers coming up the stairs, and it was used for storage." She thought about that lad, how well he'd done during the interview, his parents either side of him on the sofa in the soft room. She reckoned he'd come out of this okay, going by how he'd coped with the questions and answers, but time would tell. She hoped he didn't have nightmares and bad images floating around in his head like she did. He was young. Maybe he'd get over it more easily.

Andy rubbed a circle over his belly, which was growling. "Well, I don't know about you, but it seems we're up shit creek again with regards to being able to do anything, and there's no point hanging about here. We need sleep to be able to sort this out, and I'm bleedin' knackered."

"I agree," Helena said. "With nothing coming from the search in the woods, CCTV, or door-to-door enquiries, it seems we're stumped. Again. Let's call it a day, shall we? We've already gone into overtime. We'll look at it with fresher heads in the morning."

With computers being shut down, Helena let herself relax a bit. She longed for some food, then bed. Zach hadn't rung yet about the girls' post-mortems, so they didn't even have anything to go on there, and she hadn't had time to bug him about it. Shona and Clara had been pushed, that was a certainty, but Stephan hadn't seen it. He'd been standing beside them with his eyes closed, like the man had told them to, and the poor kid still had it in his head they'd jumped. Phil had been poking into the religious angle, specifically the phrases Stephan had recalled the man reading out from 'the crow'. Why did he call it that? And was the hollow some obscure reference like he had for the Bible?

Her head spinning with so much data, she pushed off the desk to go to her office so she could shut her computer down as well. Her phone rang, though, and she groaned.

"Wait, guys," she said, holding up a hand. "Just in case." She swiped to answer. "Yep?"

"It's me, guv." Clive.

"All right, matey?"

"Another lad has gone missing. Kid called Matty Vines. Does a paper round. Didn't come back afterwards. I wouldn't normally get hold of you about it yet, seeing as he's only an hour late, but what with the recent goings-on... I put it out on the radio, and two officers who were up there asking questions, who got waylaid at a Mrs Zadolka's about someone nicking her potted fir trees, rang in to say they saw him when he delivered a paper at her place. Matty said he had one more house to do. No one was in at the place next door when they checked. A Mr Keffler."

The hairs on the back of Helena's neck stood at attention. "Okay..."

"Mrs Zadolka said Matty delivers to his house..."

"Right. Did the uniforms go back there?"

"Yes, still no answer, so they're now looking around the area—the street, the cliff top."

"Good. Me and Andy will go to his house and check again, but it's looking likely he's away on holiday. His name has already come to our attention. Actually, we'll visit this Zadolka woman as well, then we'll go to the lad's house. Officers already there?"

"On their way. I'll let them know you'll be arriving shortly. In an hour or so?"

"Thereabouts. Address, please."

Clive gave it.

Helena thanked him, put her phone in her pocket, and looked at her team. "Sorry… Another boy has gone missing—or so we assume for the moment. He hasn't returned from his paper round. Now, as you know, normally we'd give it a few more hours, but in light of what's been happening, we need to get on this quickly." She walked to the whiteboard and swiped up a black marker. There wasn't much space left to write anything, but she jotted down Matty Vines' name and address. "So the usual, please. As you probably heard, I'll be going with Andy to Mrs Zadolka's and to check again at Mr Keffler's. After that, we'll visit the parents."

Ol flopped back into her seat, Phil sat with his head in his hands, and Evan lifted his phone off the desk, probably to ring his wife to let her know he'd be late.

"I'm just going to my office to get you some cash," Helena said. "I'll spring for dinner, so if one of you wants to order a delivery using your card, that'd be fab. I'll try claiming it back as expenses, not that I'll get anywhere, but it's worth a go."

With everyone agreeing on either kebabs or burgers from Chargrill, Helena grabbed the money, handed it to Phil, then headed out with Andy.

In the car, driving towards the outlying houses, she said, "We'll pick something up after we visit the parents, yes?"

"Yeah. Chip shop will do, won't it?"

"That's fine by me. I could eat a scabby donkey."

Andy chuckled, and that bit of levity broke the tension.

She drove up the cliff then through the estate, going a farther half mile until she reached the road where the grand houses stood on one side, quite a lot of land between them. She'd got the addresses from Evan so went straight to Keffler's, cruising up the gravel drive—no tyre tracks for a car, just foot divots—towards a home that hunched in the darkness, curtains closed.

They got out and took it in turns to knock, but it was clear no bugger was home. Next, she drove along the way a bit to Mrs Zadolka's, and the gravel leading up to her house snapped and cracked beneath the tyres. The lights were on here, including one outside, so at least this journey wouldn't be a complete waste of time.

An old woman opened the door before they'd exited the vehicle. She frowned, peering at them through the windscreen. Helena and Andy joined her on the step, and Helena showed her ID and introduced them.

"Are you here about my firs?" she asked, voice posh. "Only, the pots they're in are rather distinctive, so I'll know right away if they're mine. I planted them from saplings, and they've grown so much in a year, so someone would have needed a van to lug them off, especially with the amount of mud in the pots. Quite a weight. I told those other police officers the thief must have taken them while I was out in town earlier. I was gone for an hour and a half, so plenty of time."

"We're not here about your firs, Mrs Zadolka." Helena smiled. "We're here about Matty Vines."

"Oh, the paper lad. Yes, those officers did come back and ask if I'd seen him go past on his bike, but I'm afraid I didn't. Matty usually does the street the other way, from down the bottom up, which means I'd be the last one, but today he said he had one more, so I assumed he was going to Mr Keffler's next."

"We think Mr Keffler is away. There are no lights on, and the curtains are closed."

"I wouldn't know. I don't tend to look outside when it's dark so wouldn't have a clue if any lights come on at his. He's a lovely man, though. Goes to church quite often. I used to be friends with his grandmother, you know."

Helena gave another smile. "So you know the family well?"

"Oh yes. Mr Keffler — Francis — took over the house when his granny died — Maureen. Francis' mother didn't want anything to do with it. Something about her first husband, Francis' dad... Oh, I don't know if I should be gossiping."

"Any information you have would be great, Mrs Zadolka."

"Well, Francis' father killed himself. Jumped right off the cliff, he did. Quite the shock, and it was all over the papers. He used to have some rows and a half with his mother — that's Maureen, if I'm not being clear. Always about God and Jesus as I recall her saying. But on the contrary, the grandson, Francis, took to religion very well once he hit his teens. Such a nice chap."

"Does his home have a basement?"

"Now it's funny you should say that. Not only were policemen here, but a woman called Olivia and a man named Evan were asking about basements, and like I told them, they're cellars. I feel there's a difference. And, yes, we all have cellars along here. Mine is mostly full of junk, but I have some wonderful mementoes. Would you like to see them?"

While Helena didn't for one moment think the abductor was Mrs Zadolka, she agreed to have a quick look. Andy went down there with them, and there was no mattress, no chains attached to the wall, no Jesus picture, no wine rack, and no school uniform, shoes, and backpack. After *oohing* and *ahhing* at some ugly figurines—"From nineteen-twenty, don't you know!"—and a few mantel clocks that had stopped working over the years—"I simply can't bear to part with them!"—it was time to be getting along.

"We need to go now, but thank you for showing us your things," Helena said, making her way upstairs and to the front door. She studied a photo in a frame on the wall.

"Ah," Mrs Zadolka said. "That's Maureen and Francis."

Helena burned the image of him into her mind. Thick-set. A chubby face. Podgy lips. Clean-shaven. "Lovely," she said, although he was far from it. His eyes were positively frightening.

He reminded her of the man who'd stared up at her outside the station when Jayden had gone missing. The shape of his head was the same.

Mrs Zadolka showed them out, and Helena passed her a card.

"If you happen to notice Mr Keffler is back, please could you give me a ring?"

"Of course. Glad to be of help."

"Just a quick question. Does 'the crow' or 'the hollow' mean anything to you?"

The old lady's forehead ruffled. "Goodness me, no, only that one's a bird and the other is a dip. That's right, isn't it, a dip?"

"Yes. And thanks again."

They said goodbye and got back in the car. Helena drove past Mr Keffler's slowly, but it was still in darkness.

"What do you think?" she asked. "Can you see a 'lovely man' or a 'nice chap' doing this to these kids?"

Andy shrugged. "Some people are lovely on the outside, but inside they're blacker than sin."

"True."

She drove on towards Matty Vines' house, thinking of another person who fitted that description to a T.

"She's going to get us in the shit, boss, you mark my words." Uthway's right-hand man.

Helena pretended she wasn't awake and remained still, squashed into the corner of the storage container that was, oddly, beginning to feel like home.

"What are you fucking going on about?" Uthway said, his tone sharp and hard. "How can she get us in the shit when she's right here, with us?"

"She's a copper, and they're cunning bastards. They know exactly how to play it. She'll be making out she's all compliant, then, when you least expect it, she'll find a way to get free."

"The only way she'll get free is if we take our eyes off the damn ball, and we won't be doing that, will we?"

Helena cracked an eye open. Light from a torch on a wooden crate bathed Uthway and his sidekick, giving them a creepy vibe. They stood toe to toe, in each other's faces, and it was clear cracks were showing in their relationship. She suspected they were having a moment deciding whether they trusted one another any longer.

Not good for the type of operation Uthway was running.

"No, boss, we won't take our eyes off the ball."

Uthway had won the standoff.

"Good, because if we do and she gets away... Well, we'll have to up sticks and set up somewhere else, and you know how handy it is being based here. The sea, the boats coming in with the cargo."

"Yeah."

Helena had already guessed the 'slaves' were being brought directly here, but every time they'd been to the docks and had boats randomly searched, nothing had been discovered. She'd long since realised they were sailing in at night, in crates inside the larger vessels then departing from those very boats, probably in dinghies. The coastguard here didn't patrol all the time, neither did the police, so it would be easy to bring new 'talent' in.

She hated that word now.

Uthway didn't appear like he'd ever dirty his hands with this kind of operation. He could be *mistaken for being nice on the outside. Inside, though, he had a dark heart and a greed for money, with no care for what happened to the men and women he sold to the highest bidder, so long as precious pieces of paper with famous people's heads on them lined his pockets.*

Funny how looks could be so deceptive.

Helena jolted out of her thoughts. She'd driven to the Vines' house without registering it.

"Okay?" Andy asked, unclipping his seat belt.

"Fine, just been thinking, that's all." *About things I don't want to remember.*

"Want to talk about it?"

"No, we've got to get in that house. The sooner we do that, the sooner we'll maybe have something to go on."

Hope was a life raft, something she clung to when there was nothing left. If Matty's mum and dad had no information, Helena would be climbing aboard and praying for some kind of miracle — a cruise ship sailing by to rescue them.

Because, let's face it, we've got fuck all else to keep us afloat.

CHAPTER NINETEEN

A car was coming down the drive again. Francis spied through a tiny gap in the curtains and tried to make out if it was the same vehicle as before. It didn't seem to be. Today had been annoying for having people knock. First two policemen, then that man and woman, and now someone else.

After the first visitors had arrived, he'd gone down into the cellar to stuff a rag into Matty's mouth and tie his wrists together behind his back so he couldn't pull it out. It wouldn't be good for the people outside to hear him screaming. The stupid kid had a big mouth on him and needed to learn to keep it shut.

Francis' stomach rolled over. The people getting out of the car now… No, it couldn't be them. Surely not without asking him if it was okay first. What the fuck was he meant to do?

Quickly, he raced to the cellar door and took the key off the brass cup hook, slipping it into his pocket. He couldn't be doing with these people going down there and discovering Matty. Francis had planned to keep the kid there for a while, until the town went to sleep, then he was going to take him to the hollow and do this thing properly, like he should have done in the first place. All he needed was for about six or seven hours to pass, then he'd be undetected as he carried him through the woods.

He wasn't going to let those people in. Pretending he was out would be the best bet, then they'd have to go back home. But they were out of the car now, walking towards his front door.

No. No…

He swallowed, panic rising, and Grandmother appeared beside him at the drawing room window, hovering there.

"That's…unfortunate, isn't it?" she said, her voice shrill.

"Be quiet," he whispered. "They'll bloody well hear you."

A laugh tinkled out of her. "Don't be silly. How on *earth* would they hear me?"

"Because you're right there!" Butterflies flickered about in his chest, and he thought he might be sick.

The doorbell chimed, and he almost lost the use of his legs. Hurrying from the drawing room, he dashed into the kitchen and grabbed Jesus' blood. It tasted good as he knocked a massive swig back, and now more than ever he needed his saviour inside him, to calm, to reassure, to give him strength.

Bell ringing again, he walked to the jamb and peered around it. No, they wouldn't be able to see him, not since he'd taped brown paper over the glass in the front door. With the lights off, he was safe to walk around freely. The cellar door was beside the kitchen one, and he swore Matty's muffled squeals filtered from beneath it. It sounded as though the lad had a sore throat.

"Be quiet," Francis whispered. "Please, don't give us away."

"He's a rowdy little sausage, isn't he," Grandmother said, floating out of the drawing room and coming to stand beside Francis.

Sausage wasn't the word he'd have used. Not this self, the one who was getting angry, resentful that he wasn't being left alone today. Why had so many come? What had they *wanted*? And those at the door now…one of them wouldn't come here unless it was absolutely necessary. She hated this house.

The landline rang, and he almost dropped the bottle of blood. He clutched the neck and brought it to his lips, guzzling more down. His heart rate slowed, and finally, the effects of it smoothed out his prickly nerves. Deep breaths in and out — one, two, three — and he thought he would be all right now.

Then his mobile trilled, and he rushed to shut it up, dipping his hand into his pocket to press the OFF button. With the thing mercifully silent, he remembered Matty's phone. Had he taken the battery out of it? God, he couldn't recall.

Taking the key from his pocket, he unlocked the cellar door, then crept down there, Matty's noise reduced to grunts. He spied the phone on the floor outside the perimeter, the battery and SIM beside it.

His visitors being here had forced him to doubt himself.

Back upstairs, he locked the door again and waited.

"Why isn't he answering?" A little girl. Whining. Spoilt.

"Because he's obviously not in."

Oh, how he'd missed *that* voice, even though it was stiff, as though the woman was angry. Images of her washing up, polishing, or hoovering flounced into his head, and he had to fight with himself not to go and let her in. Mum, his beautiful, hard-working mum. But she

212

couldn't know about Matty. She couldn't be in the way of what he needed to do, and she would be if he opened that door.

"Why isn't he in?" A third voice. A boy this time.

If Francis peeked, he might catch a glimpse of his brother and sister, the siblings he couldn't recall no matter how hard he tried. Was he jealous of them so had blocked their features out? That was what Grandmother had said. The teen Francis felt otherwise — that it was better to keep those children safe, away from Grandmother, so she couldn't force him to put them in the hollow then the cellar.

He held his breath, clutching the bottle. His heartbeat was strong, too fast, so he drank some more until it evened out again. Two slams came from outside, then the rumble of a car engine. They were leaving. The Devil rejoiced, but the teen cried. He wanted to see Mum, to be cuddled, but she wouldn't do that anyway. Not since he'd found God.

Their relationship had broken down beyond repair.

So why did she come here?

He returned to the drawing room and stared through the curtain gap, just catching sight of red taillights as Mum turned the corner at the end of the drive. Would she come here tomorrow? That would be okay, Matty would be in the hollow by then, but when it came time to put him back in the cellar, Mum would need to be gone.

Could he risk letting her in if she knocked again in the morning?

Going in the kitchen, he finished the dregs of blood and opened a new bottle. That would be his comfort while he waited until he could take Matty to the woods.

Jesus was good. Jesus loved him.

Matty had never been so frightened in his life. Mr Keffler had turned all weird on him, forcing Matty down into the cellar, punching him in the face when he'd screamed for help.

"Shut it," Mr Keffler had said, "or I'll have to hit you even more."

Matty had ignored him and screamed again, and the second punch had hurt so bad he'd cried. The third stunned him into silence, and he fell, landing on a mattress. Mr Keffler had forced him to take his clothes off, except for his pants and socks, then ordered him to put on this freaky dress and massive slippers. Then he'd chained him up, switched on a little brass lamp, and left him alone.

Since then, several knocks had sounded upstairs, and at first, Matty had thought it was Mr Keffler banging about, but his brain registered the specific noise, and he'd known someone was at the front door. Had Mum got worried when he hadn't come home and had called the police?

He'd shouted out again, and Mr Keffler had come back down, stuffing a disgusting piece of material in his mouth then tying his hands behind his back. Matty had almost gagged until he reminded himself to breathe through his nose and concentrate on that instead of what was happening. When Mr Keffler had gone back upstairs, Matty rose, running forward in an attempt to break the chains off the wall, to get to his phone on the floor, planning to use his foot to bring it towards him, but all that had happened was him snapping back and landing on the mattress again, his wrists barely escaping being broken.

Mr Keffler had said he'd be reading from the crow soon, and Matty had no idea what that could be. He hoped it wasn't a real bird, because he'd been scared of them ever since a seagull had landed on his head and pecked at it when he'd been five or six. It had dug its claws into his head.

He shivered at the memory.

He grew tired, his eyes drooping, and despite trying to stay awake, he couldn't fight it anymore. Fear had weakened him, so he flopped onto his side on the grey blanket, which didn't smell very nice. He closed his eyes and hoped, when he woke, that this had all been a vicious nightmare.

It wasn't.

A man came down wearing a balaclava — Mr Keffler? God, it was so frightening, and Matty almost wet himself. The man sat cross-legged on the floor, opened a black book, and stared at Matty.

"Here is the crow." Yes, it was Mr Keffler. "Listen carefully, as these are your first words that will guide you to a better life."

Francis glanced at the clock. Ten. It would have to do. He couldn't stand to hang around any longer.

He rose from the table and slid his bomber jacket on, pulled the balaclava into place, and attached his head torch, keeping it off for the moment. Although Matty knew who he was, he hoped by going down into the cellar with his face covered again, Matty would think he was someone else.

He unlocked the door and went down the steps, the brass lamp's light even more meagre than usual. The batteries probably needed changing. Matty was asleep, snoring slightly — probably because he undoubtedly had a broken nose from Francis punching him — so Francis busied himself checking his backpack. Torch. Rope. His keys. A hammer and a small tub of nails. The note he'd written to tack on the wall. Paint and a brush. He lifted Matty, draping him over his shoulder, then hung the backpack strap over the other.

The boy didn't stir.

Must be knackered.

Francis crept upstairs, left the house, secured it, and walked up the hill. Mrs Zadolka would be in the Land of Nod by now, so she wouldn't see him slinking by. He rounded the corner past her cloaked-in-darkness house and headed towards the cliff top. Matty was heavier than the other two, or maybe that was 'dead weight' talking. The woods came into view, and he rushed towards them, Matty's head bouncing, banging against Francis' back.

Still the lad didn't wake.

Once under the cover of trees, Francis relaxed and slowed a bit, switching on the head torch. The hollow was in the centre, and another five minutes saw him there. He placed Matty on the ground and undid the padlocks, then tugged the circle out of the hole. It took ages to cuff the boy to the cross, Matty once again flung over his shoulder, but now he hung like Jesus, head bowed, appearing dead and defeated, his skin a weird silver colour in the light of the head torch. Francis took the paint and brush out of the backpack then popped the lid. He painted stigmata on Matty's palms, and Jesus sang inside Francis' head.

He joined in. "I once was lost, but now am found, was blind, but now I see."

There. Matty was perfect now.

Francis hammered nails into the two top corners of the message, then packed his things away and stepped out of the hollow, leaving the brass lamp on. Finished securing the circle, he started for home, content, sure this was going to turn out exactly right.

It didn't take a brainbox to work out Dad had jumped off the cliff, what with all the kids at school whispering about it and teachers giving Francis sad looks. He hated it that they'd been told and he hadn't. Mum had just said he was 'gone', not how or why, and he decided he'd believe her, not everyone else.

Although the knowledge that it was true reared its head over the years, each time, he stuffed it away. Every so often, he went to stand on the cliff in Dad's spot, and now was one of those times. He'd had a hard day at school, and yesterday Grandmother had forced him to recite passages from the crow, and he'd forgotten a line, and she'd taken Grandad's slipper to his backside.

Life was too much, and if it wasn't for making sure Grandmother didn't stop giving Mum a bit of shopping money every week, he'd have told her to stuff God and Jesus up her arse a long time ago. Terrified of doing so, not wanting Mum to cry, the sound of it filtering through their dividing bedroom walls like it'd done when Dad had gone, he promised himself he'd keep going until he could go to work and provide the cash for her himself.

He was due at Grandmother's so turned away from the jostling water and walked to the place he would call home sometime once she was dead, so she kept saying. If he did as he was told. He liked the idea of Mum living where she didn't have to pay rent or a mortgage.

He knocked on the door, and Grandmother answered, staring at him as though he'd done something wrong — which could be anything from a big misdemeanour to a small one.

"Get in here, you imbecile," she said, grabbing the lapel of his school blazer and hauling him inside.

"What's the matter?" he asked.

"Last time you were here, what happened?" She shut the door and let him go, glaring at him in the darkened hallway.

"I…I messed up reciting the Bible."

"You did. You also promised never to do that again, but Father Pinto told me you even did it there last night when you were helping with one of the teen gatherings. What sort of example is that?"

"I'm sorry, Grandmother."

"Well, it seems you can't be," she snapped. "Yesterday's whipping didn't teach you a thing. Perhaps you need another, and this time, you'll do it to yourself."

"No…please…I…"

"Be quiet, cretin."

She shoved him down the cellar steps and taught him how to self-flagellate. He must remember the Bible quotes, he must remember the Bible quotes…otherwise, she said, he would have to do this to himself every day until he did.

Years Later

Wrecked from her treatment of him, he still hadn't broken free of Grandmother's insidious hold. And he knew he never would. Too much had happened, too much had been drilled into his head by the woman who, by rights, should be a kindly influence in his life but, instead, was a wicked old cow who'd created a monster inside him.

At twenty-three, he'd almost thrown himself off the cliff, but the thought of Mum going through pain held him back, as always. Father Pinto had asked Francis to lead the choir now the old bloke who usually did it had admitted defeat and retired, and it gave Francis something to look forward to, what with living alone in Grandmother's house now and having no friends.

She'd always said Jesus would greet her at the gates when she died, but he hoped she was in Hell with the Devil. How she managed to appear in real life he didn't know when he knew damn well she was dead.

"There will be plenty of lads to choose from there," Grandmother had said when Father Pinto had offered him the job.

"No. I'll be one of the first people they look at if one of the choir boys go missing. Father Pinto would come up on the radar, too, and you wouldn't want your precious priest questioned, would you?"

He hugged himself, once again standing there in Dad's final place, and wished the man had some balls and had stood up for himself, taken his family away from Grandmother's influence.

"What, like you should do?" the teen side asked. "Shouldn't you grow some balls?"

"Leave me alone."

His foot slipped, and he let out a scream and windmilled his arms, struggling for balance. He pushed himself back, then fell, landing on his arse and staring out at the sea, his heart palpitating.

No, he wouldn't be growing balls or saving himself.

He was too far gone for that.

Matty woke again, only this time he wasn't in his own bed or on the mattress in that room at Mr Keffler's place. He stared ahead at a wall with a piece of white paper attached to it, scared shitless that he seemed to be in some kind of little wooden dome.

The note said: *Remember the words of the crow, and all will be well.*

Matty shook his head; the movement jiggled his hands. Something tinkled, and he glanced to the side. Short chains. Attached to the wall above. A small lamp hanging on a hook. He still had the weird dress and slippers on, and his shoulders and arms ached from his position.

Mr Keffler had always struck him as weird, but not *this* weird. Maybe Matty was in a shed of some sort in the bottom of Keffler's garden. Would he die in here, forgotten?

He cried and couldn't stop.

CHAPTER TWENTY

Mr and Mrs Vines were understandably worried, and once Helena had questioned them, she asked Dave to come over and go through the procedure with the distraught couple.

"We'll do everything we can to find Matty," Helena assured them at the door, rubbing Mrs Vines' arm.

"I promise you, he really isn't that sort of kid," Mrs Vines said. "I would never have rung the police if it had been our Rowan; I'd have expected her to be late. But not Matty."

"I understand. You know your child best." Helena didn't like the usual spiel they were told to give, undermining what a parent said about their sons or daughters. They were the ones who'd brought them up, so who were the police to brush the claim aside that it was out of character for the missing person to behave that way?

"I do." Mrs Vines wiped her eyes. "And with what happened to Jayden and Stephan…"

"Try not to think about that. I know it's hard, though. Go inside. Dave will help you through this. We'll be in touch either directly or through Dave. Bye for now."

Helena walked to the car, glad to be out of their house — the atmosphere had been so fraught it was stifling. She drove to the chippy, Andy silent beside her, and parked outside it. Ferreting in her glove compartment, she pulled out some money, passing it to Andy, and he got out, leaving her in peace for a few minutes.

She contemplated the interview with the Vines, then recalled Matty's room, which was ordinary, complete with his haphazard style of dumping clothes on every available surface until Helena hadn't been sure what was clean and what was dirty. They'd found nothing of interest to further their investigation, which left them to rely on his digital footprint on the Web, his phone records, and any CCTV that might have captured an image of him.

She rang Evan and asked him how that was going.

"It's taking a while for the phone records to be released. We have Matty entering then leaving the newsagent's where he collects the papers before delivering them. Rogerson's."

"Ah, Mr Pickles," she said.

"Why does everyone call him that, d'you know?"

"Nope. One of life's mysteries. Where did Matty go after that?"

"Left out of the doorway. He got on his bike and turned it around, heading towards the cliff top. Of course, the camera cuts off at the end of the street, so where he went after that was provided by Pickles, who gave me the addresses of the people who buy the paper. I rang them, and they remembered the time it was delivered, and Keffler isn't in, so…"

"Okay, so the timing works out, yes?"

"Yes. The last house was Keffler's. I've been in touch with uniform, and they've been enquiring at houses on the nearest estate, but so far, no one has seen Matty."

"Unless he went home via the cliff top," Helena said. "His mother warned him not to go there or to the park. Kids, eh?"

"Don't," Evan said. "I've got all this worry to look forward to when mine grow older."

Helena chuckled and stared through the windscreen at a man acting suspiciously on the other side of the road. "Hang on a sec. I've just got to watch this bloke a minute."

"Where are you?"

"Outside the chippy in town. Andy's in there getting our dinner."

The man had a dark bomber jacket on, a black polo neck, and black slim-fit trousers. He paced up and down, glancing at his chunky watch every so often, acting agitated as fuck.

"You okay?" Evan asked.

"Yeah, I just need to get a good visual on his face." Her heart pumped extra fast—the shape of his head was familiar.

He walked with his back to her, then turned and…

"Fuck!" Helena said. "Get backup down here. Now!"

She dumped her phone on the passenger seat and shot out of the car, legging it towards him. For a second, he stopped and stared at her, and in that time she got a bead on who he was, except he had a trendy beard now and longer hair, but she'd recognise those eyes any day.

"You fucking arsehole!" she shouted.

He laughed then swivelled, running up the street.

Helena gave chase, the strength to nail this fucker fuelling her, flushing away the weariness she'd experienced since this afternoon. With every pound of her feet on the pavement, thuds

226

jolted through her. He sped up, and she followed suit, determined to catch up with this piece of scum.

"Stop! Police!" she called now a few people had appeared, coming out of a pub up ahead.

He dashed in there, and she dived in after him, getting jostled by people left and bloody right. He shoved through the crowd—why was it so fucking busy?—leaving her way clear as people parted to let him pass. At the back, he pushed through a door marked PRIVATE, and she lurched after him, banging her shoulder on it as it moved to close. She caught sight of him hauling his arse up some carpeted stairs.

A squeal came from above, and Helena took the steps two at a time, her leg muscles burning from the sudden burst of exercise, lactic acid building. On the landing, one door was open, and she vaulted inside, stopping short at the sight that greeted her.

A kitchen with a dining area ahead. The man. A woman in front of him. He held the blade of a knife to her throat and stared at Helena over the woman's shoulder, his eyes glinting with evil intent.

"Back off, bitch," he snarled, "or I'll slice this silly cow, and it'll be all your fault."

In her peripheral vision, Helena spotted someone peering around the doorway at the back. There seemed to be a living room on the other side, but she couldn't be sure. No matter. Backup would be here soon.

"Put the knife down," Helena said, maintaining eye contact. "You're not doing yourself any favours, you know that." Her legs went to jelly at his piercing stare, and she stiffened her spine to give off the aura he didn't scare her.

If he thought she was frightened, it was game over.

The scent of rancid sweat wafted towards her — terror coming out through pores.

"Please don't hurt me," the woman said, looking at Helena as though she was her guardian angel, pleading with her eyes to be saved. "I've got money up here in the safe. You can have it, and there's more downstairs. My husband will get it."

"I don't want your fucking money," the man ground out. "I just want you to *shut up*." Spittle flew from his mouth.

The person in the other room entered the kitchen on silent feet. He was big, beefy, about mid-forties, and held a baseball bat. Helena kept her attention on the couple in front of her.

For the bat bloke's benefit, she said, "My name is DI Helena Stratton, and I order you to put that knife down."

"Order!" The bearded bloke laughed and pressed the knife closer. "Fuck off, skank."

The woman shrieked, her eyes widening, her breathing heavy.

A whiff of cooking oil took Helena's sights off them for a moment. Tendrils of smoke wavered upwards from a pan on the hob. "I need to turn that burner off or there'll be a fire. You can see the smoke, can't you?" She looked at the knife-wielding man again.

He nodded. "Do anything stupid, and she's dead. Got it?"

Helena held her hands up and sidled to the left. She kept her gaze pinned to the couple and reached out to move the pan off the heat, praying she didn't upend it and pour hot oil on the naked gas flame. "Why are you involving an innocent person?" She remained where she was, the warmth from the cooker top burrowing through her jacket.

"You didn't give me much choice."

"Oh, you had a choice. You could have kept running. Didn't have to come in here, did you," she said. *Two more steps. The other man's nearly there…*

"You'd have caught me, and I couldn't have that. Can't allow myself to be brought down by the likes of *you*." He sneered.

That sneer was wiped away, replaced by a frown, his mouth sagging open, and a shout barking out of it. He lowered his hand from the woman's neck, dropped the knife, and clutched at his head where the baseball bat had smacked into it. Then he went down.

"Back off," she said to the bat user and leapt forward, shoving the woman to the doorway Helena had entered through.

Then she was on her knees behind the man, pulling her cuffs out of her jacket pocket, hardly able to believe she'd be using them on him. The scent of his body odour was overwhelming and almost her undoing. But not quite. She was stronger now.

Staring at the bruised lump burgeoning on the back of his head, she said, "Jason Uthway, I am arresting you for the crimes of sex trafficking, abduction, unlawful imprisonment, rape, and murder. You do not have to say anything…" She continued speaking until what she had to say was out, adrenaline buzzing through her, relieved that it was over and he was right there. Right. Fucking. *There.* "Why did you come back, eh? Thought you could start again just by keeping out of sight for a few years? You absolute knob."

The air-splicing wail of sirens sounded like heaven.

"Fuck off," he said, voice strained.

"Got a bit of a headache, have you?" Helena smirked. "Funny how being whacked like that can bring one on, isn't it?"

"Suck my cock, bitch."

230

Don't let the memories come back now. Fight them.

Feet thundered on the stairs, drawing her away from teetering on the ledge inside her head. Clive and another officer came barging in, and the frightened woman stood by the door, shaking and sobbing, clutching the jamb, her knuckles white. The man with the bat walked past to comfort her.

"Get this bastard away from me," Helena said, rising but keeping hold of Uthway's wrists, hating the skin-to-skin contact.

Clive came and gripped Uthway's upper arm. "Oh, we've been waiting to see you again. What a sorry sight. You're going to be a treasure in the nick. Nice muscled man like you. You'll be the star of the show."

Helena smiled. "Lots of people *road testing* you. Seeing if you're good enough for the *highest bidder*." God, she hated him.

"Up yours," Uthway said. He spat on her cheek.

She managed not to cringe. "Thanks for the DNA sample. Most appreciated."

While Clive shoved Uthway downstairs, Helena took a moment to lean against the wall and close her eyes. Of all the times she'd envisaged bringing him down, it hadn't been like this. She'd thought she'd arrest him in her house, in her bedroom, where he'd kept to his promise to come for her.

She opened her eyes, and the other officer handed her a tissue.

"Thanks," she said, wiping her cheek.

Two more uniforms arrived, and she stuffed the Kleenex in her pocket and rushed to the sink to wash her hands and face—scrub that bastard off her. She left the officers to sort out the man and woman and take statements. Downstairs, she pressed through the bodies in the pub, the scene before her surreal, everyone going about in slow motion, drinks being raised, mouths opening in laughter to show toothy smiles. The music from the old-fashioned juke box sounded tinny, but she made out the words just fine.

"Yes, I'll survive now all right, Gloria Gaynor," she whispered and pushed open the pub door.

Time sped up, sensations and sounds slapping at her—people talking inside, coppers speaking on the path to her right, the cold air cooling her hot skin, the hairs all over her body rising. Lights flashed on top of two police cars. Inside the back of one was Uthway, gazing out at her, licking his lips like the goddamn pervert he was. She gave him the middle finger and turned away, not allowing him the satisfaction of knowing he could still give her the creeps and get under her skin.

Andy was legging it towards her, clutching parcels of fish and chips to his chest, his tie flapping over his shoulder. Helena laughed, and it sounded hysterical. Manic. Like she was mad. She threw her head back and let the relief pour out of her, hoping Uthway watched her and hated her for finding this all so funny.

"What took you so long?" she asked, finally getting herself under control.

"They had to fry the damn fish. Took a sodding age." He came to a stop in front of her, panting. "What are you bloody laughing at?"

Him asking that nearly set her off again. She felt free — at last. It didn't matter that a trial was coming up in the future. She'd give evidence, all the while knowing it would put Uthway inside for a long stretch.

"And what the fuck's going on in there?" Andy tipped his head towards the pub. "Bar brawl or what?"

"I got him," she said, looking into his eyes. "I fucking got him."

"Thank God for that. How? Was it Keffler? Did he say where Matty is?"

Helena shook her head. "Not him. I haven't got that one yet."

"Who then?" He frowned, pulling his chin back in thought.

"Uthway," she said and walked off, heading for her car, euphoria winging its way through

233

her veins. "Now maybe I can start properly living again," she whispered to herself.

"Hey, wait up," Andy called. "I know we go to the gym, but I'm no marathon runner yet."

She laughed again, this time normally. He caught up with her, and they walked side by side in the middle of the road.

"I can't believe you bloody nicked him. How do you really feel?" he asked, putting an arm around her shoulder.

It was warm from where he'd held the chip packets.

"At the moment? Fucking buzzing," she said. "But I know that might change. Still, for now, I'll take it. Plenty of time for doubt to seep in."

"There shouldn't be any," Andy said. "We know it's him who organised everything. We have all the evidence stacked up and waiting. All we needed to do was find him. D'you reckon he came back to start again?"

"Of course he bloody did." She opened the driver's side door, relieved her phone was still there and the vehicle hadn't been stolen. Her keys dangled in the ignition.

They got in and ate their dinner, watching through portholes in the steamed-up windscreen as a meat wagon came to collect Uthway. Good. He needed the proper treatment, not being ferried to the station in the comfort of a car. She swallowed a chip, thankful she wouldn't have to interview him. Her involvement with Uthway meant someone else had that pleasure, but she'd watch the recordings when she got the time. At the moment, she had a young lad to find—and he was more important than her seeing Uthway acting bolshy in an interview room, a place she'd dreamt of him being for too long now.

Food eaten, she balled up her paper and threw it in the back seat. Andy did the same, and she opened the window to get rid of the condensation on the glass. A thought hit her, and she rang Ol.

"Listen, we're going to Keffler's again to do a bit of surveillance."

"Okay, guv. It's all the usual here. We're poking into things. Social media is pretty quiet—Matty doesn't use it much. Oh, and we had a call from one of the local papers. People have been talking about the lads going missing."

"Bloody wonderful. I knew that would happen eventually. What did you say?"

"I did the standard: *We're unable to comment at this time*. That okay?"

"Perfect. I'm thinking of hanging about at his place until about two."

Andy groaned.

"Oh, and someone we've been looking for will be turning up at the station soon. Give it ten minutes, and you might want to go down and watch him being booked in." She ended the call before Ol could ask who it was.

Setting off for the outlying houses, she drove with a smile that hurt her cheeks. She'd finally got the bastard who'd tried to ruin her life. Now she was going to find the one who'd ruined other people's.

CHAPTER TWENTY-ONE

Francis came out of the woods and made for Dad's spot on the edge of the cliff. The wind was up, pushing him to the side a bit, and when he stood right on the tip of the land, a stiff breeze almost shoved him over.

Was that God, angry with him?

Jesus' blood still warmed his veins, and if Jesus no longer loved him, it would be cold, wouldn't it?

Yes.

The sea, choppy and angry, gushed about below, churning, asking him to dive in, like it always did, so it could guzzle his body. He took a step back, afraid, and looked down, his head torch illuminating his shoes. It was okay. He was on solid ground. Despite that, he moved back another few paces and studied the sky with its heavy-bellied clouds tinged with black. A storm was on the way then. He'd better get home before the rain started.

The walk across the cliff top was bracing, the fresh air invigorating, and he took it to mean he'd turned a corner in his mission—it was going to work out, it really was. It didn't take long to reach the strip of homes outside the estate, and he walked past Mrs Zadolka's at the top of the hill then went down towards his house.

Grandmother waited for him ahead, her hair flying like it had some other time, but he couldn't remember when now. She folded her arms below her breasts and tapped one foot, clearly angry, clearly about to give him what for.

He was so tired of her. So weary.

"Why don't you just fuck off?" he said, approaching her, the Devil pushing the words out of his mouth.

"Is he locked up in the hollow now?" she asked. "Did you leave it exactly as it should be?"

He walked past her, and she lumbered to keep up. He dared not say he'd left the brass lamp on inside the tree.

"Yes." He sighed.

"Good. Leave him this time. Don't go back there until the forty-eight hours are up."

"Yes, Grandmother."

He strode on, leaving her behind, intent on getting home so he could open a new bottle of Jesus' blood. It would help him to sleep. He had just enough time to pull this off before he had to return to work and normality.

What a mad few days it had been so far.

No sooner had Helena parked down the road a bit and doused her lights than a circle of white ahead bobbed midair.

"Someone's coming," she said. "With a torch." She pointed up the road. "Zadolka wouldn't be out at this time, surely."

What if they'd misjudged the old dear and she'd been the one to take the boys?

"It's a bit hard to tell who it is with only two streetlamps out this way." Andy leant forward and peered through the windscreen.

The white blob got bigger, the person getting closer, and Helena made out the shape of a man as the figure drew level with Keffler's house. It looked as though the torch was on his forehead.

"That him, do you reckon?" she asked.

"Yep. He's going up the drive, look."

"Let's go."

Helena and Andy got out, and they ran across the road, slowing upon reaching the drive. The man was halfway up it, so Helena dashed forward. He spun around, and the light blinded her. She lifted her hand to shield her eyes, and Andy came up beside her.

"Mr Francis Keffler?" Andy asked.

"Get back," Francis said. "You're the Devil's work, being out this late. No good will come of you roaming in the darkness."

What the fuck?

Helena blinked to clear away the bright dots seared into her retinas.

"I'm DS Andy Mald; this is DI Helena Stratton. We'd like a word."

It was frustrating not being able to see his face to check whether mention of the police had freaked him.

"Let me get the crow, and I'll give you some beautiful words," Francis said. "The Lord would like you to listen. Jesus says it's okay."

Helena's guts contracted. *The crow.* "Sir, I'm going to switch my own torch on." She unclipped it from her belt and lit it, pointing it at his face.

A fucking balaclava.

Her heartrate went a bit crazy.

"Where have you been this evening?" she asked, her voice thankfully calm, although inside she was raging. It had to be him who'd taken the boys. Too much of a coincidence otherwise.

"I went to Dad's place."

"And where's that?"

"On the cliff top."

"How often do you go there?"

"Most nights."

"Did you happen to be there when two girls were pushed off, by any chance?"

He glanced to the side. "Fuck off, you."

"Who are you talking to, Mr Keffler?"

"My grandmother."

Helena moved the torch that way. "There's no one there. Was her name Maureen?" She shifted the beam back to him.

He blinked. "Yes, and she is there, talking to me. Always talking, telling me what to do." He lifted his hands to his head.

She sensed Andy stiffen.

"Hands down by your sides," Andy snapped.

"Stop speaking," Francis said. "I won't listen to you anymore. Go away. I need blood. I need to drink some blood."

Helena's mind spun. *Blood?*

"It's *her* fault you're here," he went on. "If she didn't make me... No! I *will* tell them. This has to stop, you hateful old cow!"

"Where is Matty Vines, Mr Keffler?" Helena asked.

He appeared to struggle internally, like he was having a battle with himself. "In the...in...the... No. Get off me." He batted at the air, then fell to the gravel on his back, fighting with an unseen enemy.

He was testing Helena's patience, acting as though he had mental health issues. "I've fucking had enough of this," she said quietly to Andy. "I used my cuffs on Uthway. Do the honours, would you?"

Andy pushed Francis onto his side and cuffed his wrists. "This is a precaution for our safety, as you appear to be agitated, Mr Keffler. Now get up." He helped the man to stand. "Where is Matty Vines?"

"In the hollow," he whispered.

If she heard that word one more time... "And where the fuck is *that*?" she ground out.

"In the...in the woods."

"Dump him in the bloody car," she said, rage building. "We'll get him to show us."

On the walk to the vehicle, she rang the front desk and asked for backup, saying she'd wait for them at the tree line on the cliff top side.

"Send an ambulance, too, just in case," she said.

Andy put Francis in the back seat, sitting beside him, and she drove up the road then turned left down the side of Mrs Zadolka's — sod the fact she was on the grass. Taking another left, she sped along the cliff top, glancing in her rearview every so often, catching glimpses of

Francis' mouth moving, low mumbles coming out of him. Andy's face showed his contempt.

At the edge of the woods, she braked to a stop and got out, ordering Francis to do the same. She gripped his arm and led him towards the trees. "We'll wait here for a moment."

"She's followed us," Francis said. "She's standing right behind you."

"That's lovely for her," Helena said, not in the mood to play games. "Did you hurt Matty?"

"I had to punch him."

"Had to?"

"Yes. I didn't want to do any of it."

"Get that sodding torch and balaclava off him," Helena said. "They're getting right on my tits."

Andy moved to the car and brought out two evidence bags. He slipped gloves on and removed and bagged the items, putting them in the boot. Helena lifted her flashlight and shone it in Francis' face. Fleshy lips. Strange eyes, which had a haunted look about them.

"Did you kill Jayden Rook?" she asked.

"No. He died by himself."

"Why did you leave Stephan Korby here on his own, blindfolded and bound with rope?"

"Grandmother told me to kill him, but I couldn't, so I let God decide."

She took a long breath through her nose. "Decide what?"

"Whether he died or not."

This bloke was beginning to sound properly whacko. She didn't think it was a put-on anymore.

"Do you believe in God, Francis?"

"Of course I do. I have to, otherwise she'll…put me in the hollow and the cellar."

"God wouldn't want you doing these things. You know that, don't you? He isn't unkind. He wouldn't want you being cruel."

"Yes, but she said— I'm warning you, old woman. *Piss off!*"

Two police cars came from the way Helena had driven. They parked, and Clive got out of one. She wished there were more uniforms to be had, but unfortunately, the ones on duty were spread thin at the best of times, due to the cuts. Clive and the other officer, Brent, she thought, walked over. An ambulance arrived then, and they all trooped through the woods, Helena, Clive, and Brent using their torches. Around five minutes passed.

"Here," Francis said, pointing to an oak.

It had the widest trunk she'd ever seen.

"*This* is the hollow?" she asked.

"There are keys in my pocket."

"Andy," she said.

Andy retrieved them. "What are they for?"

"The padlocks and the cuffs." Francis dipped his head, his shoulders shaking.

244

If he was bloody laughing, she'd be hard pressed not to punch the fucker.

Clive went over to the tree and moved to the side of it. "Look at this, guv."

Helena waited for Andy to hold Francis' other arm, then she let him go and strolled over. There were four padlocks attached to small metal arches.

"Get the key off Andy, will you?"

Clive put gloves on, took the keys, and returned, opening the padlocks. He pulled at the arches, and a large circle of the trunk came away. Faint light spilled out, illuminating the front of Clive's uniform. He bent his head a little and stared inside. "Are you all right, lad?"

Jesus Christ. Matty?

Helena quickly put gloves on and stood beside Clive. "Oh God. Don't worry, love, we'll get you out of here very soon." She took the keys from Clive and said quietly in his ear, "Get that wanker away from here. I don't want the boy seeing him. Take Brent with you, and see if the meat wagon's available again yet."

Clive nodded.

"Where am I going?" Francis asked.

Helena glanced his way, then stepped inside the hollow. Just the name of it gave her the bloody creeps. She looked at Matty. The poor kid was hanging by his wrists, exactly how Stephan had described. She called for Andy, and he came inside—a bit of a tight squeeze, but she needed him to hold the lad up while she unlocked the cuffs.

"We're police officers, okay?" she said to Matty. "I'm Helena, and this is Andy. We're going to get you down, all right?"

He nodded, and a sob tore out of him.

It sounded like an animal.

"Andy here is going to hold you up. Is that fine by you, because he'll need to touch you?"

"Yes," Matty whispered.

"Then I'm going to unlock the cuffs. The man who did this to you has been caught, so there's no need to worry."

He cried then, and she worked as quickly as she could, tears of her own falling down her cheeks, her damn throat closing up. The terror these boys had been through...

Fucking hell, get a grip.

Andy carried Matty outside, and Helena left the hollow, sick to her stomach, and walked a few metres away while the paramedics checked Matty over. She pulled her phone out and rang the front desk.

"It's Helena. I need SOCO down at the woods at the top of the cliff. About a five-minute walk in, they'll see us if they get here quickly enough."

Then she called Ol. "We've found Matty, and it was Keffler."

"Oh, brilliant." She told Phil and Evan, and a cheer went up. "Is he hurt?"

"I think he's fine physically, but mentally, he's shaken up, which isn't surprising. He was hanging inside a fucking tree. That was the hollow."

"*Inside* it?"

"Yes. Someone had carved the damn thing out."

"What?"

"I know. SOCO are on the way, and thankfully we don't need Zach. What I *do* need is for you lot to go home. There's nothing more you guys can do tonight that can't wait until tomorrow. Me and Andy will be a while yet. And did you go down to the front desk to watch the booking?"

"We all did. Well done, you. How do you feel?"

"I'm well happy but at the same time livid at Keffler."

"I can imagine."

"I need to get on. See you in the morning."

"I'm glad for you, guv. You know. For *that* to be over."

Uthway. At last. "Me, too. Now sod off home." Next, she called Dave. "We've got him. Matty and the abductor. Mr Keffler."

"Oh, brilliant. All well?"

"As it can be. Paramedics are with him now. He'd been kept inside a tree, can you believe that?"

"Dear God."

"Right, well, don't pass that on to the parents for the moment. Just let them know he's okay, and we'll meet you all at the station in a bit. I'm just waiting on SOCO to check this tree and the surroundings."

She ended the call and took a couple of minutes to just stand there and absorb the scene. Matty had a white blanket around him, covering an ugly green dress. He had tartan slippers on and, thanks to Stephan's statement, there was no doubt Keffler was the man who'd abducted all three boys. The paramedics were asking questions, their voices gentle, and she admired their dedication in ensuring the poor kid was at ease.

She turned to face the way they'd come in. Lights bobbed in the near distance, and a troop of people in white suits got closer. She walked to meet them and explained what they'd find.

"Unfortunately, we didn't put booties on. That's my fault. My mind was on finding the child."

"No problem," Tom said, his smile bright in the light of her torch.

"You'll also need to go to Keffler's address." She told him what it was. "The kids were kept in

248

the cellar there. I have keys here. I assume one of them will be for the house."

Tom took them. "Brilliant."

She showed them the tree, then walked to the stretcher the paramedics had placed Matty on. They carried it, one in front, one behind, and Helena and Andy strolled either side. Matty held his hand out, and Helena took it, the lump returning to her throat, the tears reappearing in eyes that stung. His palm and fingers were freezing.

"We're taking you to the station, Matty, but your mum and dad should be there by the time we arrive."

He didn't say a word, and she wondered whether he wouldn't fare as well as Stephan. Everyone coped with trauma differently, and she hoped once he'd had a good sleep and lots of hugs from his parents, things might not bother him so much.

There was that hope again. Always there.

CHAPTER TWENTY-TWO

Francis had a psychiatric evaluation, so Helena wouldn't be speaking to him anytime soon. He'd chatted with the psychiatrist, Lesley Duran, in the soft interview room, though, with the video running.

Helena watched the recording on a computer monitor a day or so later. Francis had been taken to a secure unit for more tests. It was looking likely he wasn't fit to stand trial at the moment. Lesley had told Helena to fast-forward to the two-hour fifteen mark.

On the screen, he sat on the sofa, hugging himself.

"Who are you now?" Lesley asked.

"The teen side."

"I see. And how do you feel when you're the teen side?"

"Frightened. So afraid for Mum. She can't manage. Grandmother pays for our shopping. If I don't go to church, she'll put me back in the hollow then the cellar—and she'll stop buying our food. I don't want Mum to go hungry."

Bloody hell…

"What else does your teen side feel about what Grandmother did to you?"

"I want to get away from her. I don't like her." He jolted, his body spasming, and flung his arms away from his body, resting his hands beside him. He curled them into fists.

"Who are you now, Francis?"

"The Devil." He glared at Lesley, eyebrows scrunched. "And those fucking kids should be dead. They lived and got me in the shit."

"But when the detectives spoke to you on your driveway, you partially admitted what you'd done, so isn't that yourself you should blame, not the children?"

"That was the teen twat talking."

"I see. Are there any other sides of you?"

"There's another, but he's the one who does everything she wants. Grandmother. She was in the hollow and cellar, too. And she put her own kid in there. My dad."

"Why did she do that?"

"To make us love God and Jesus. I need the blood. I can't go without the blood."

"What is the blood, Francis?"

"The blood of Christ. I need to drink it so Jesus is inside me. I'm the child in the tree. The child in the tree."

Helena switched it off. She'd had enough. From what she'd gathered from Lesley and just by watching that short interaction, Francis Keffler had created multiple personalities in order to cope with what had happened to him. Each side represented his various blocks of feelings, and he assigned those feelings to what he saw as actual new versions of himself in order to express whatever he was going through at any given time. She thought about how it must have been awful for the teen side to come into play when he'd been holding the boys hostage.

He also believed he saw his Grandmother, who he said could visit him from Hell. He spoke to her frequently, usually in a mean way, so he did understand that she wasn't a good person, yet at the same time he'd obeyed her.

The human mind was too complicated for Helena to fathom, but at least now Francis would get the help he needed — and no more boys would go missing.

She took a deep breath and reached for her coffee, dawdling on purpose. On the night

Uthway had been arrested, she'd relished the thought of seeing his interview, but now she'd had time to think about it—and had starred in a particularly harrowing nightmare—she wasn't so sure.

If she didn't, she'd be forever asking herself questions. Best to just rip the plaster off and be done with it.

She accessed the file and switched it on.

Uthway sat beside his solicitor, a man of about sixty who looked like he charged a fortune for his services, going by the Rolex on his wrist and his sharp, navy-blue suit, white shirt, and red tie with a gold pin keeping it in place.

Andy and Evan sat opposite him, Evan leaning back with his hands folded over his chest, Andy leaning forward, all business.

"We're here to ask you questions about your sex trafficking business. We have stacks of evidence, so it's pointless denying it," Andy said, playing bad cop. "Photos of you entering Lime Street, where we found a room jam-packed with people who had been raped and were destined to be sold to men with a lot of money who wished to use them as sex slaves."

"What a load of old bollocks," Uthway said.

"Not according to DI Helena Stratton."

"*That* slag? She was begging for it. She asked me to fuck her. And my mate."

Helena almost pressed pause. Nauseated, she swallowed and covered her mouth with her hand.

"So you admit to having sex with Miss Stratton?" Andy asked.

"I'm sure you've got the evidence of it, seeing as she's a copper and all." Uthway looked bored.

"Where did the encounter occur?"

"Dunno. A hotel somewhere."

"So not in a metal storage container on the cliffs, where your DNA was obtained from a spill of semen?"

"Not fucking likely." Uthway chuckled. He didn't seem perturbed at all.

"What about your semen being found inside Miss Stratton, at the Lime Street address, and also from a sample given by Emilija Yatvik, who, it was clear, had extensive damage in her vaginal area."

Helena winced. Emilija was one hell of a brave woman.

"Never been in Lime Street," Uthway said. "It must have been planted there. That Emilija would have done it — whoever she is."

"Why would she do that? Why do you think she would run naked from Lime Street?"

"God knows. For effect. All them foreign bints are mental, aren't they?"

Helena shook her head. The man didn't give a shit.

She didn't need to hear any more. Everything would come out in court—all the people found in Lime Street were willing to testify. That bastard wouldn't see the outside of a cell for a very long time.

Switching the video file off, she went upstairs. Instead of going into the incident room, she strode to Yarworth's office to give him the cursory update. He never acted interested when she told him about cases—and he wasn't to be bothered when she was working one either. Another man who didn't give a toss.

Helena knocked on the door.

"Enter!"

She walked in, and he held his hand out, indicating the seat opposite him. She sat and told him what had been happening, the telling taking twenty minutes.

"Two arrests in one night," he said. "My, you are good."

Is he taking the piss?

"I have to say," she said, "we would have been swamped if we didn't have Evan. I heard you're moving him elsewhere. If that's the case, sir, why bother bringing him in to begin with?"

"I've changed my mind on that," he said, placing his pen on the skin between his upper lip and nose, moving it from side to side. "He makes the station look good. Things get done faster with him around."

Charming. She couldn't say they'd done it just as well without him, otherwise Yarworth might get rid of him after all. Evan was a part of their work family now, and she'd miss him if he left. "Good. He's exceptional."

"Anything else?"

"No." A tiny part of her had expected him to ask her how she felt with Uthway being caught, but she should have known he wouldn't care. Still, it hurt a bit. He was her boss and should be concerned as to whether she could keep it together on the job. She'd force him to acknowledge it. "I'm going for private counselling again. Two months, once a week."

"Why's that then?"

God, he was insufferable.

"Seeing Uthway has reminded me I still have a few demons hanging around. Only little ones. Nothing I can't get rid of."

"Fair enough. Anyway, off you go. I have to go out and have dinner with the mayor."

You absolute, unfeeling bastard. "Have a nice time, sir." *Choke on your steak, sir.*

She left the room and the station, on her way to her own dinner. Zach was waiting for her in The Blue Pigeon. It felt like she hadn't seen him for days, when in reality it had been on the cliff with the girls' bodies a few days ago. In the meantime, she'd had to catch up on sleep and do a ton of paperwork, and now she felt more human, she'd agreed to have a bite to eat with him.

In the incident room, she looked around at the empty desks, her team long gone, home and relaxing after a particularly harrowing case. Evan had dropped Andy off to save Helena doing it, and she sighed at how well she got along with her partner now. All those years they'd stuck it out, getting on each other's nerves, Helena always going off by herself and not including him. Andy letting himself go after his wife, Sarah, had left him. Now, with the gym training, he was fitter and happier, and his relationship with Louise was going from strength to strength.

Tomorrow, they'd all be back here, working hard, putting things right.

She wouldn't have it any other way. This was her life, her calling. Zach was fast becoming her life, too. With Uthway caught and Marshall in prison, maybe she could now come to terms with her hideous past and move forward, allowing her heart to fully let Zach in.

Helena switched off the light then turned and walked out, down the stairs, and into the car park. She breathed in the cold night air and looked at the stars, pleased she was free to see it while being outside, whereas Uthway and Marshall would only ever catch a glimpse of it through a small, high window.

With another chunk of weight lifted from her shoulders, she got in the car and headed for home, where she quickly had a shower and changed her clothes. She walked to The Blue Pigeon—it was only a short distance away—and pushed the door open. Inside, she glanced towards their favourite table, and there Zach was, sitting there looking over at her.

She grinned and rushed to him, feeling so free of old burdens and the wicked torment she'd been through. Free to love this man without borders or boundaries. He stood and hugged her, and she pulled back to stare at his face.

"I bloody love you," she said, eyes misting.

"Blimey, where did that come from?" He laughed and rubbed the tops of her arms. "Did you manage to watch the tapes? Are you okay?"

She nodded, overwhelmed with gratitude that he'd asked. That he cared.

"I did. I got him, and I got the other one, and now I can rest easy."

She sat, as did Zach, and they held hands over the table.

"I'll pay for this meal," she said.

"I should think so after you left me with the bill in the Indian." He smiled.

She reached over and poked him in the ribs. "Oi, you."

Yes, she could definitely rest easy, living a life free of worry and trauma.

And it was a bonus that she'd found the original child in the tree.

Printed in Great Britain
by Amazon